MURDER AT THE LEANING TOWER

T. A. WILLIAMS

Boldwood

First published in Great Britain in 2024 by Boldwood Books Ltd.

Cover Design by Nick Castle

Cover Photography: iStock and Shutterstock

A CIP catalogue record for this book is available from the British Library.

Paperback ISBN 978-1-80483-257-8

Large Print ISBN 978-1-80483-258-5

Hardback ISBN 978-1-80483-259-2

Ebook ISBN 978-1-80483-255-4

Kindle ISBN 978-1-80483-256-1

Audio CD ISBN 978-1-80483-264-6

MP3 CD ISBN 978-1-80483-263-9

Digital audio download ISBN 978-1-80483-262-2

Boldwood Books Ltd
23 Bowerdean Street
London SW6 3TN
www.boldwoodbooks.com

To my lovely granddaughter, Iris, who deserves a black Labrador in her life.

1

WEDNESDAY 11 MAY – AFTERNOON

'What do you think about the political situation here in Italy, Oscar?'

Oscar didn't reply but I didn't really expect him to. It was an unfair question for two reasons. First, with something like fourteen different political parties in play, trying to decipher the complex matrix of coalitions in the Italian parliament would be no easy task even for a dedicated academic. The other reason it was an unfair question is that Oscar is a Labrador.

All I got in response was a single eye that opened, checked I wasn't offering him food, and then closed again. I gave him a gentle prod with my foot. 'All right, politics isn't your thing. I get that. What about football? How do you think Fiorentina are going to get on next season? This season, they've just been middle of the road. Do you see any improvement coming, Oscar?'

It's funny the things you find yourself thinking about and talking about when you're on a stakeout. I can remember numerous such occasions, particularly in my early years in the Metropolitan Police, when I had to spend long, tedious hours staring through a camera lens or a pair of binoculars at a suspicious house, vehicle or gathering. On the cases when I had company, the topics under discussion rarely moved beyond sport, sex, TV and then back to sport again. As I had risen up the ladder to Chief Inspector, I had gradually spent less and less time out at the sharp end and more time back in the office. Now that I had resigned from the Met, moved to Tuscany, and set up my own business as Dan Armstrong, Private Investigator, I once again found myself doing my own legwork, and it wasn't always a bundle of fun.

I uncrossed my legs, raised my arms up above my head and stretched my back. My fifty-seventh birthday was coming up next month and I was beginning to feel my age. Oscar, on the other hand, was only three years old and full of vim and vigour – although you wouldn't have known it if you'd seen him that day laid out at my feet snoring quietly to himself. We were squatting in a tiny broom cupboard belonging to Florence's *Università degli Studi*, keeping careful watch on one particular window of the physics department on the other side of the quadrangle, waiting to catch a certain physics professor in flagrante with one of his students. My all-singing, all-dancing camera with its amazing, long, telephoto lens was set up on a tripod, trained on the scientist's window, ready to capture any goings-on in the laboratory. As with so many of the cases I had been handling recently, marital infidelity was yet again the name of the game – although I knew full well it was no game.

Outside, it was another beautiful spring day here in Florence. In fact, back in England, we would have called it a perfect summer day with the temperature already in the high twenties, even though it was still only the middle of May. There was no ventilation in our little closet but the thick, stone walls of the five-hundred-year-old university building did a pretty good job of keeping the worst of the heat out. Even so, I knew that my dog and I would both be glad to get outside again once our job was done.

It took another hour before our work was completed and I had shot off twenty or thirty highly compromising shots of the couple in question lovingly entwined on a table between a computer and what might have been a laser. I hoped they would be careful alongside such potentially lethal equipment, although the laser was probably going to be the least of the professor's problems now. I had no doubt that this would be ample proof for the unhappy wife who had engaged me to spy on her husband. I packed the camera and tripod into their bag and stood up. Oscar, realising that our mission was complete, jumped to his feet and shook himself. I reached down and ruffled his ears.

'How does a walk and a drink sound?'

From the expression on his face, it sounded just fine.

After a short walk through the tortuous streets of the *centro storico*, I stopped at my favourite bar just along from my office for a beer for me and a bowl of water and a biscuit for Oscar. It was quite a narrow street, with cars parked nose to tail all the way along the other side, but even they failed to spoil the sheer beauty of the Renaissance façades. I sat at a table on the pavement and watched the world go by as I so often do. Florence has got to be one of the most cosmopolitan places on the face of the earth, with its never-ending influx of tourists, and I often play the 'guess the nationality' game. I had already reached ten definites and another half-dozen not sures when my phone started ringing. It was Lina, my invaluable personal assistant, researcher, receptionist and friend. We had known each other for almost two years now and, although she had only been working with me for less than two months, she knew me all too well.

'*Ciao*, Dan, would I be right in thinking that your job at the university has finished and you're sitting somewhere not too far from here?'

'With a cold beer in my hand, yes, Lina, you got me. What's

new?'

'There's a gentleman here to see you. He's English and he doesn't speak Italian.'

Lina had been learning English for some time now but I could tell from her voice that she was feeling a bit insecure, so I hastened to down the last of my beer. 'I'll be there in two minutes.'

When I got back to my office, I found myself confronted by a tall, young man, probably little more than twenty-five or twenty-six years old, wearing a black leather jacket, black rollneck and black jeans. Considering that most of the people I had been watching outside in the street had been wearing shorts and T-shirts, he must have been boiling hot. He rose to his feet as I came in and immediately took a step backwards as he spotted Oscar. I was quick to reassure him.

'Don't worry about Oscar. He's as good as gold. Sorry to have kept you waiting. How can I help you?'

With a wary glance in the direction of Oscar, who was looking mildly offended and had pointedly turned his back on my visitor so he could sit down and scratch his ear with his back leg, the young man came over to shake my outstretched hand. As he did so, he produced a business card from his pocket and handed it to me. 'Piers Cooper-Stevenson. I'm pleased to meet you.' His accent wasn't quite the royal family, but it was pretty posh all the same. I saw his eyes flick across towards Lina at her desk and he lowered his voice. 'What I have to speak to you about is highly confidential. Is there somewhere secure where we can talk?'

'My office is through there.'

I opened the door and waved him in, making sure that Oscar went straight to his basket rather than bothering the young man. As I followed him inside, I glanced at the business card. It had a logo of what might have been a bird of prey and simply *GS Flight*. His name was below it, followed by *MA (Oxon), MBA* and his job title was *Business Development Executive*. I checked him out more closely as the two of us sat down by the window overlooking the medieval courtyard on the fancy armchairs that Anna had insisted I should buy. Anna is my girlfriend and, like many Italians, she has an eye for style, regardless of cost. Still, business for Dan Armstrong PI had been pretty good lately so I had meekly agreed and shelled out the money and had to admit that the chairs looked good.

Piers Cooper-Stevenson was a bit of an enigma. With the jeans and the rollneck, I mentally pigeonholed him as most likely being involved with the media, maybe the music business, TV or cinema but, with that accent, he could have been a future member of parliament. What, I wondered, had brought him here to Florence? Business or pleasure? From the visiting card, I presumed it was the former.

It was.

No sooner had he sat down than he leant forward towards me, still keeping his voice low. 'Please can you confirm that you are Dan Armstrong, formerly Detective Chief Inspector Armstrong of Scotland Yard?' He was sounding unexpectedly formal.

I nodded. 'The very same. What can I do for you, Mr Cooper-Stevenson?'

He looked reassured. 'Piers, call me Piers. You come highly recommended. We hope we can count on your help.'

'It's always good to be recommended; can I ask who gave you my name?'

'Miss Selena Gardner, no less.' His tone exuded gravitas as he basked in the reflected glory of the world-famous actor's name. 'She told us you're the best in your field anywhere in Europe.'

I smiled at the Hollywood hype. I had met Selena Gardner the previous year when I had been involved with a particularly puzzling murder case. In spite of being one of the richest and best-known actors on the planet, Selena had turned out to be a warm, generous person – as well as stunningly beautiful – with whom both Anna and I had struck up an unexpected friendship.

'If I can, I'll be delighted to help, but you'll have to explain what you'd like me to do.'

'How well do you know Pisa?'

I looked up with interest. The famous city of Pisa was just over an hour's drive away from Florence. 'I've been there a couple of times as a tourist – to see the Leaning Tower and so on – and once on business, investigating a missing person. I don't know the city anything like as well as I know Florence, but let's say I'm reasonably familiar with it. Why Pisa?' I gave him an interrogative look and he picked up his story again.

'My boss is hosting an important meeting there in two weeks' time and he'd very much appreciate it if you could be responsible for security while the meeting's taking place.' He put his hands together and looked past me out of the window, almost as if he was praying. 'Is that something you would feel able to do?'

My immediate reaction was to shake my head. 'It was very kind of Selena to recommend me and it's kind of your boss to think of me, but I'm a private investigator, not a bodyguard. What sort of security is he hoping to obtain? And security from whom? If he thinks any of his guests might be in danger, then I would recommend getting proper security guards. I can give you the name of a good firm here in Florence if you like.'

He reached for his briefcase, set it on his knees and opened it. From it, he produced a sheet of paper and handed it across to me. A quick glance revealed that it was a familiar form: a non-disclosure agreement. My eyes ran across the first few lines of complex legalese relating to the limiting *of all information which might fairly be considered to be of a confidential nature and includes, but is not limited to...* I didn't bother reading on. I had seen enough of them in my career and almost knew the wording by heart by now. I raised my eyes again.

'I'm going to need some more information from you before I sign an NDA. First of all, what sort of security are you looking for? Like I said, I don't offer a bodyguard service.'

'Not that sort of security. What we need is the assurance that nobody's listening in on what will be highly confidential discussions.'

That sounded more like my sort of work. 'Can you assure me that the meeting in Pisa will be completely legal and above board? Where is it taking place, who are the participants going to be, and what exactly is the nature of the meeting? Although I'm no longer on the force, there's no question of me getting involved with anything illegal.'

Piers shook his head in what looked like genuine horror. 'Good Lord, no, absolutely not. My boss would never dream of anything like that. I can assure you that there's nothing illegal going on. It's just that this meeting is very sensitive and very secret.' He paused as he searched for his words. 'The people taking part are all major players in the field, some household names, and if news of what's being discussed at the meeting were to get out, there would be hell to pay.'

'When you say major players in the field, what sort of field are we talking about?'

'Ours is a media company and the people in Pisa are mostly involved with financing a new project, a major one. I can't tell you more until you sign the NDA.'

'And why's the meeting taking place in Pisa? Are the people who'll be participating in the meeting based in Italy?'

He shook his head. 'No, none of them. It's very much a UK affair. Italy was chosen because it's neutral territory.' He produced a hint of a smile. 'And the food's good. My boss likes his food.'

'Tell me, where exactly will it be taking place?'

'In Pisa, like I say, in a private villa a little way out of town. We have use of the place for a week. It belongs to somebody known to my boss and it comes highly recommended as being both comfortable and secluded. It'll be staffed entirely by people who've signed NDAs just like this.'

'And how long will the meeting last?'

'Five days, starting on Monday, 23 May.'

'Right, let's see if I've got this straight: your boss – whose name has not yet been disclosed to me – is hosting a meeting, or a series of meetings, later this month, strung out over a bit less than a week to discuss some confidential matters and he wants to be sure they aren't overheard or disturbed.' I saw him nod. 'And you can assure me that nothing that will be discussed will be illegal and none of the participants in the meeting will come from a criminal background?'

He nodded again, vigorously. 'Absolutely. This is a high-level business meeting. So, will you sign?'

'One more question: does your employer want me just to check the place out and do a sweep for bugs and so on, or does he want me to put in an appearance?'

'He would like you to give the villa an initial health check and then stay on for the full duration of the meetings to monitor the situation, just in case news might leak out and spark unwelcome interest from outside. The villa's self-contained with bedrooms, dining and living areas and kitchens. There's a separate apartment in the grounds where you would stay. If you want to bring your wife or partner, my boss said he would have no objection as long as they also agree to sign an NDA.' He pointed across the room to where Oscar was rolling about on his back in his wicker basket, which was making sinister creaking noises under his weight. 'And there would be space for your dog as well if you like.' He allowed himself a moment of levity. 'There would be no need for him to sign an NDA.'

'I'm sure that'll come as a considerable relief to Oscar.' I stood up. 'Can you give me a moment to speak to my assistant? She has control of my diary. Would you like a drink of something?' I glanced at my watch and saw that it was almost half past five. 'There's coffee or tea or I've got some cold beer in the fridge if you prefer. The coffee's Italian but the tea's English.'

'To be honest, a cup of tea would be very welcome. Milk, no sugar, thank you.'

I opened the door and looked out at Lina, who was at her desk. 'Could we have two teas, please, milk, no sugar, and could you check the diary for later this month, in particular the week of the 23rd?' Because I'm old-fashioned, I was still operating with an actual diary made of real paper and written on by hand although Lina had been bullying me for weeks now to let her set up a proper schedule on the computer. I knew I would have to give in sooner or later but, like I say, old habits die hard.

Back in my office, I quizzed my guest a bit more. Understandably, he was unwilling to give me any more detail of the meeting participants or any concrete idea of the nature of the agenda until such time as I had signed the NDA. What he did tell me was that most of the people involved in the discussions – five of them including his boss – would be accompanied by their partners and there might be one or two gophers like him. He used the word 'assistants' but the meaning was the same. Top-level execs usually need somebody to go here and go there, doing the running about for them, looking after their everyday needs. Mind you, I told myself, I was a fine one to speak. After all, Lina now fulfilled almost exactly that function for me.

Lina brought us in our teas along with the diary and stopped to talk me through the entries for that particular week. The upshot was that with a bit of juggling, we worked out that I should be able to commit to spending the week of the 23rd in Pisa. I waited until she had left again – not because she's untrustworthy, but because my young visitor had obviously been told to keep disclosure to a minimum – before telling him I could manage to free myself. He looked relieved and I wasted no time before breaking the news to him that my services for a full week weren't going to come cheap. To his credit, he didn't bat an eyelid when I laid out my terms but then, of course, it wasn't his money he was spending.

I made a copy of the NDA for Anna – in the hope that she could get away to accompany me – then signed mine and passed it back to him. 'Now, first things first: who am I working for? What exactly is GS Flight?'

'GS Flight is a subsidiary of the Grunstock Media Corporation. The head office of GMC is in LA but GS Flight is based in the UK and I work out of the London office. The CEO of GS Flight is Malcolm Derby, but the founder and owner of the parent company is Alexander Grunstock. He's based in LA. I imagine you've heard of him.'

I had indeed. I remembered reading an article that described Alexander Grunstock as *more powerful in the media world than Rupert Murdoch and Warner Brothers put together*. His Grunstock Media Corporation owned some of the most influential – and lucrative – film and TV companies around the world. My visitor's unquestioning acceptance of my terms was now explained. I almost wished I'd quoted a bit more.

'Yes, I've most certainly heard of GMC, although your company's not familiar to me.'

'It's a very new company, but I have no doubt you'll be hearing a lot more about us very soon.'

This sounded intriguing, but for now, I stuck to the basics. 'I'm going to need details of the exact location of the Pisa villa. When can I get access to the place? When are the first guests likely to be arriving and, indeed, when will you and Mr Derby be arriving? Also, how sure are you that none of the other people involved in this meeting won't spill the beans about it taking place or reveal what's going to be discussed?'

He nodded several times. 'It wouldn't be in anybody's interests to leak details to the media yet.' He looked up from his teacup and caught my eye. 'I mean that, seriously; we're talking about something very new and potentially revolutionary.'

'I don't want you to go into any detail, but can you at least give me an idea of what you mean by that? I need to know who might want to listen in.'

Piers set down his cup on the coffee table and cleared his throat. 'I'm afraid I'm not authorised to tell you anything about the specifics of the agenda, but I can tell you that this project, if it goes forward, could potentially put people like Sky and the BBC out of business – and that's just in the UK. Worldwide, the effect could be huge.'

'You mean you're creating a whole new way of delivering the news?'

'Not just the news: everything from movies to gameshows, documentaries to concerts.' He caught my eye. 'In other words, almost anybody involved with television anywhere in the world would be prepared to give their eye teeth to eavesdrop on the discussions. That's why we need your expertise.'

I nodded. 'I can see how dearly the UK media would love to get hold of a story like that, but at least we aren't talking about anything involving international criminals or terrorists. I think we can assume that Mr Derby is more worried about cameras and microphones than he is about explosive devices or armed assault.'

'Exactly, in particular coming from rival media companies.'

'And you think they might go so far as to bug the premises?'
This sounded a bit OTT.

'All's fair in love, war and business.' He shot me a little smile.
'That's one of Mr Derby's favourite sayings. After all, the UK
tabloid press has made a bit of a name for itself doing just that.'
The smile melted away as he returned to more serious matters.
'You mentioned sweeping for bugs. Can I take it that you have
access to sophisticated anti-bugging equipment?'

I nodded. Only a few weeks earlier, I had invested quite heavily
in a professional-quality scanner, which claimed to be able to
locate the most sophisticated listening devices as well as hidden
cameras. While researching exactly what to buy, I had been
amazed to discover that cameras now existed that were smaller
than the tip of my finger and microphones almost imperceptible to
the naked eye, all of them capable of transmitting the information
they recorded directly to a receiver – often little more than a smart-
phone – a considerable distance away.

'Yes, I should have adequate equipment to ensure that the
property's swept clean before the meeting starts, although I would
need to keep doing regular sweeps throughout the week, just in
case one of the people attending or a member of villa staff
manages to smuggle something in.' I held up my hand to stop him.
'Yes, I know what you're going to say. It's not in the interests of the
people at the meeting to reveal what goes on, but it's best not to
take any chances.' I saw him give a rueful nod of the head.

'Yes, of course. You know best, I'm sure. As far as I know, Mr
Derby and I will be arriving on the Sunday evening. I'll check, but
I believe you should be able to get access to the villa from that
morning, if you think that'll give you enough time to get everything done.'

'That should be fine. Now, let me have all the details, starting
with the address.'

2

WEDNESDAY EVENING

I went round to Anna's house just before seven and found her slumped on the sofa looking drained. She works as a lecturer in Medieval and Renaissance History at Florence University and I knew that the last few weeks had been particularly stressful for her. From what she'd told me, she'd been having an uphill battle with the faculty head to get approval of her proposed curriculum for the following year. I gave her a hug and a kiss while Oscar gave her his usual boisterous welcome.

Anna and I had been going out for over half a year now and things were going really well between us. I lived in the little house I had bought the previous year in the Tuscan hills, about twenty minutes outside Florence, and she lived in her lovely apartment in a historic building not far from the Ponte Vecchio. We had been spending more and more time together either here or there and the wonderful thing about her flat was that it was barely a five- or ten-minute walk from some of the most famous sites in the city, and the whole place was redolent with history. The best part about my house was the fact that it was set amid vineyards and olive groves on a hillside dotted with cypress trees, and the views from the house were exceptional all the way across the valley of the River Arno and on to the distant Apennines beyond. It also offered wonderful walks for me and my four-legged friend.

'*Ciao*, Dan, how was work today? Oscar, you're a lovely dog but get off me, will you? You weigh a ton.' She eased him off her lap and waved vaguely in the direction of the kitchen. 'There's beer and wine in the fridge if you like, but I don't think I can summon the energy to get up.'

I sat down beside her and took her hand in both of mine. 'I'm fine, thanks, and my day was okay – the usual snooping and spying. I've got a bit of news which might interest you, but first of all tell me about your day. How's the fight with the dean going?'

'I'm getting there. Right now, we're just arguing about whether Leonardo da Vinci or Michelangelo should occupy the number-one spot.'

'My money's on Leonardo, but what do I know? Are you sure that's all that's bothering you? You do look troubled tonight.'

She gave me a little smile. 'You detectives are too clever for your own good. Yes, I am a bit troubled. I had a phone call from Virginia this afternoon.'

I had yet to meet her daughter, the product of Anna's marriage to a Brit, which had ended in divorce ten or eleven years previously. Virginia had been born in the UK where Anna used to work and she was still living there now. She hadn't been back to Florence since Anna and I had got together the previous autumn. I knew she was a very bright girl who had got herself a first from Oxford and that she was a year or two younger than Trisha, my own daughter, but that was about all I knew of her. Her mother rarely spoke to me about her. I waited for Anna to explain. It took a while before she finally came out with it.

'She called me this afternoon to tell me that she's coming over to Tuscany later this month on business...'

Her voice tailed off and I did my best to help. 'That sounds good. Is she coming here to see you?'

'Yes and no.' Anna was sounding decidedly awkward. After another pause, she finally decided to come clean. 'The thing is, she says she wants to see me, but she doesn't want to see you.'

'Ah...' All became clear. I had introduced Anna to my own daughter at Christmas with a certain amount of trepidation but the two of them had hit it off wonderfully. Trisha was still very close to my ex-wife, but she had embraced the new woman in my life remarkably willingly. She appeared to be genuinely happy to see me happy. Divorces are tough on kids and I could understand Virginia's hesitation but, surely, after ten years, she had to accept that her mum had every right to start again. I did my best to reply diplomatically, trying to keep the mood light.

'I can't say I blame her. If I was somebody else, I probably wouldn't want to meet me either.'

'It's all very well for you to joke about it, but it's important to me that my daughter meets you and realises why I fell in love with you.'

I gave her a little peck on the cheek. 'My youthful good looks and boyish charm, I expect.' Even Oscar looked up from the floor in disbelief at this and I hastily returned to more serious matters. 'It's not really one of those things you can put your foot down about, though, is it? Just give her time. Sooner or later, curiosity will get the better of her. How is it she's coming to Tuscany on business? Does she do a lot of travelling for her job? Come to think of it, what is her job?'

'She works for a big finance company in London – they do everything from building multimillion-dollar dams in developing countries to producing new anti-viral drugs. They don't actually do any of those things; they put up the capital. She says they're now moving into the media.'

I nodded. 'Sounds amazing. I would imagine they make a healthy profit on deals on that scale.'

'From what I can gather, the whole empire is owned by just one man and he makes an absolute fortune. She hasn't worked there for long and she's still finding her feet but she says the scale and variety of their operations are phenomenal. Since starting work there, she's already travelled to the US, South America and South East Asia. They're truly global.'

'But this will be the first time to Italy?'

'Yes, the meeting's being organised by a big media company.'

'A big media company, did you say?' A loud bell started ringing in my head. 'This visit to Tuscany, it wouldn't be to a villa in Pisa by any chance, would it?'

Anna looked up in surprise. 'Yes, it is, but how did you know that? If I didn't know you better, I'd say you've been bugging my phone.' She gave me a wink. 'Don't tell me you've started spying on me as well.'

'I would never dream of it, sweetheart; I'm far too much of a coward to risk your wrath. No, it's just a coincidence.' I went on to tell her about my visitor this afternoon, although without revealing too much detail about the reason for the meeting coming up in two weeks' time. I finished up with an invitation. 'The man I saw told me that they want me to stay at the villa for the full week and he said that I can bring Oscar and a guest if I like. The only thing would be that you'd need to sign a non-disclosure agreement in case you overhear any confidential stuff. I've already signed one. What do you think? That way, you could see more of Virginia. How busy are you going to be the week of the 23rd?'

I could see that she was still taking in the significance of this coincidence. My brain was also whirring, just like hers. It now appeared clear that Virginia was going to meet me whether she liked it or not, so would it be better if she met me with her mum or without? Clearly, Anna was thinking the exact same thing.

'I'll still be working all month, so the most I could do would be an afternoon or two, but I would then have to get a train back to Florence that night or very early the morning after. The thing is, like I told you, she's just said she doesn't feel ready to meet you, but of course now, like it or lump it, that's exactly what she's going to have to do.' She gave a frustrated sigh. 'If you feel like getting up, a glass of wine might help us think.'

I went through to the kitchen and opened the fridge door. It came as no surprise to find that Oscar accompanied me. He had been here to Anna's apartment often enough to know exactly what delights lay inside the fridge and which cupboard alongside it held his special dog biscuits. I pulled out a bottle of cold, white wine and filled two glasses. Under the unrelenting stare of the dog, who was unsuccessfully attempting to give the impression that he was in the later stages of starvation, I dug out one of his big biscuits and gave it to him.

Back in the living room, I handed Anna her wine and picked up the conversation again while Oscar settled at our feet and crunched his way through the giant, bone-shaped biscuit. 'She's your daughter and you know best, but I think you'd better warn her in advance. If she really feels so strongly about not wanting to meet me, maybe she can speak to her boss and swap places with somebody else in the office. After all, a week in Tuscany would probably appeal to most people.'

Anna took a mouthful of wine and nodded her head. 'You're right, she needs to know.' She shot me a little smile. 'Virginia's very ambitious. From the way she was talking earlier, being selected to accompany her boss on this trip is quite a step up for her. It'll be interesting to see whether ambition triumphs over emotion or vice versa.'

'What's the name of her company?'

'JXF Finance. She works for the CEO, a dynamic thirty-something called Jonathan Farmer.'

Now, why was that name familiar? I found myself scrolling back through my ageing memory banks to remember. I was cheered to find that it took barely a matter of seconds. I remembered it only too well. There had been one of those investigative documentaries on TV that had described Jonathan Farmer as Britain's youngest self-made billionaire, although serious doubts were raised in the programme about exactly how he'd managed to do so well for himself. Interviews with people who claimed to have been swindled by his company hadn't stopped the ruling political party at the time from accepting hefty donations from him, though. The TV programme had ended with an ominous question mark, but it was looking very unlikely that Farmer's company would ever face formal investigation. One thing was for sure: he had some very influential friends and very deep pockets.

'I've heard of that guy and he's absolutely loaded, although not everybody says nice things about them.'

Anna nodded. 'Virginia says she went into it knowing his reputation and she's been trying to keep an open mind for now, although she doesn't think too highly of the big boss. She told me that even if she moves on in a year or two, having worked there will look good on her CV. She was head-hunted from her previous job and they're paying her about twice what I make.'

'Well, good for her. And now she's coming over to take part in what sounds like a very high-level meeting.'

'That's what she told me.'

'She must be very good at her job.' At least, I hoped that was it. Ever suspicious, I wondered if maybe the dynamic thirty-something might be whisking her off to Italy for a reason other than her ability in the office. The TV documentary had hinted darkly at Farmer's antics as an inveterate womaniser. Wisely, I didn't voice my doubts to Anna.

Although Anna offered to prepare food – she had already sampled my attempts at cooking and had very sensibly taken over most of the duties in the kitchen as a result – I insisted on taking her out for a pizza. We went to our familiar pizzeria, in a tiny piazza just across the Arno heading towards the Piazza del Duomo, and we sat outside on the pavement with Oscar sprawled at our feet. It was a warm May evening and I didn't even need a jumper, although occasional buzzing by my ear reminded me that the mosquito season was already beginning. I ordered a *pizza ai frutti di mare* while Anna opted for a mixed salad with prawns and olives.

As we ate, we talked over the whole Pisa and Virginia thing and Anna promised to call her daughter as soon as she got back to the flat to break the news to her that I'd been engaged by the organisers of the meeting. I told Anna the name of the villa where the meeting was going to be taking place and to my surprise, it rang a bell with her. She checked on the Internet, found what she was looking for, and read it out to me.

'The Villa Gregory is just outside Pisa and it was built in 1897 by Thomas Elias Gregory, a wealthy industrialist from Manchester, England. The villa is built in the style of traditional Renaissance Tuscan villas. It remained in the Gregory family until the outbreak of the Second World War, was used by German and then American occupying forces before being sold to another Englishman, Lord Augustus Cornish. It's still owned by the descendants of Lord Cornish today.' She looked up from her phone. 'Listen to this; this is why I remember the name. I love this story. Thomas Gregory

often boasted to his friends in England that from his bedroom
window, he could see the Leaning Tower, even though it was in fact
hidden from sight by a slight rise in the otherwise flat Pisan coun-
tryside. When some acquaintances from his London club questioned whether this was really the case, he hastily ordered the
construction of a one-sixth-scale replica of the tower – complete
with the 5.5 degree lean the original had reached before remedial
work to stabilise it – at the far end of his estate and sent photos to
each of them, just so that he wouldn't lose face.'

I shook my head in disbelief. 'That was the sort of thing the
mega rich used to do. For all I know, they maybe still do it today. By
the sound of it, your daughter's boss could probably afford to build
a full-size replica of the tower if he wanted. Still, the villa sounds
like quite a place. I'm sure you'll enjoy it if you come along.'

'I'm sure I would under normal circumstances, but I'm just
bothered about how Virginia's going to react to coming face to face
with you.'

'How old is she now?'

'Twenty-eight, almost twenty-nine.'

'Well, that means she's old enough to be able to make up her
mind. You said she's a bright girl, so I'm sure it'll be all right.'
Although I was doing my best to sound positive and encouraging, I
wasn't looking forward to the confrontation that awaited me in
Pisa.

Any further discussion of the subject was interrupted by the
sight of a couple of familiar faces. Lina and her husband had
clearly had the same idea and had come out for a pizza as well.
This wasn't completely unexpected as it had been Virgilio, Lina's
husband, who had introduced me to this pizzeria in the first place.
He was the head of the *squadra mobile*, the Florence murder squad,
and his career so closely mirrored my own that we had formed a
lasting friendship ever since I first arrived here in Tuscany. I some-

times helped him out, particularly if a case came up involving English speakers.

I waved to them and invited them to join us. The waiters rallied round and swiftly added another table and two chairs alongside ours so that the four of us could sit together. Virgilio sat down with a sigh and leant back in his chair, enjoying an affectionate greeting from Oscar, who knew Virgilio as well as he did Lina.

'God, what a day! Some crazy woman hit her husband over the head with a cast-iron frying pan and then pushed him off the balcony of their sixth-floor apartment. No prizes for guessing why she was so unhappy with him.' He gave a helpless shrug. 'She discovered he was carrying on with another woman.'

'Just so long as he wasn't a physics professor at the university.' Only a couple of hours earlier, Lina had sent the professor's wife the compromising photos of him carrying on with his student. I had expected these to result in divorce, but hardly murder.

'No, a bus driver. In fairness, it wasn't a complicated case. His wife made the mistake of pushing him to his death in full view of a couple sitting on the balcony of a neighbouring block. It was just so senseless.' He sighed again. 'What is it about some people?'

Over our dinner, I told Virgilio that I had been engaged to keep an eye on a group of top-level business people in a villa in Pisa later that month and he offered a bit of advice.

'Hopefully, you won't fall foul of the police there but, if you do, try to steer clear of a guy called Vinci.'

'Not Leonardo by any chance?' I grinned at him over the rim of my beer glass.

He shook his head. 'Adolfo – like Hitler – and he's pretty similar to his German namesake. He's an inspector in the murder squad and he fancies himself as a tough guy, like one of those bad Hollywood cops. He even carries a Colt 44 Magnum around with him at all times. He likes to think he's a character from a movie –

although he doesn't have Clint Eastwood's looks.' He caught my eye and winked. 'Anyway, as long as you don't kill anybody, you should be all right.'

'Thanks for the warning, but I have no intention of killing anyone.'

3

SUNDAY 22 MAY – MORNING

I arrived at Villa Gregory at just after nine o'clock in the morning. It was a fine day and from the cloudless sky, it looked as though it was going to be a hot one. After an unusually dry winter, Tuscan farmers were crying out for rain, but as far as I could see, they weren't going to get their wish today.

I approached the villa along a dead-straight road with pan-flat fields stretching away on either side into the distance, as usual here in Italy without hedges dividing them one from another. Poly-tunnels and umbrella pines were just about the only things to break up the uniformity of the landscape. Ahead of me lay the forest, reed beds and lakes of the Parco Regionale Migliarino and beyond it, the sea. Anna had told me that back in the Middle Ages, most of this land here would have been underwater and Pisa itself had been a major sea power. As the River Arno and two smaller rivers had gradually washed more and more sediment down with them, the area had gradually silted up and it was now rich farmland.

Surrounding the estate belonging to the villa was a high, brick wall, almost submerged beneath a dense canopy of greenery, and I was unable to get so much as a glimpse of the house within. Clearly, the residents of Villa Gregory liked their privacy. I pulled off the road and stopped in front of a pair of tall, forbidding metal gates. There was a letter box and what looked like an intercom set into the left-hand pillar, so I climbed out and went over to it. I pressed the bell and waited, and waited, and waited. Finally, there was a crackling sound and I heard a voice.

'Who's that?' It was a male voice speaking Italian and he didn't exactly sound warm and welcoming.

'My name is Armstrong. I've come here to do a security check of the villa.'

His response, had we been in England, would probably have been *Harumph*. As it was, he produced one of the numerous colourful expressions in the Tuscan vocabulary to express dissatisfaction.

'Porco Giuda...' This was followed by a heartfelt 'Oof' sound but then, at least, a yellow light on top of the gatepost started flashing and the gates began to open. I returned to the van and cast a look over my shoulder to where Oscar was on his feet behind the back seat, a hopeful expression on his face.

'Somehow, I don't think we're flavour of the month with this gentleman, Oscar. We'd better be on our best behaviour.'

Once the gates had opened fully, I drove in and followed a gently curving gravel track through at least twenty metres of dense undergrowth and trees before emerging into the open. Here the track widened into a large parking area formed around a charming fountain with a pair of stone nymphs set at its centre. Beyond the parking area, at the end of a short path and up half a dozen stone steps, was the front entrance of the villa.

If Anna hadn't told me that it was little more than a hundred years old, I would have had no difficulty in believing that I was looking at a Renaissance original. It was perfect in every aspect of its design, from the faded red roof tiles to the dusty, dark-green, louvred shutters on the multitude of windows. It was a three-storey building, painted in the classic, Tuscan, light-ochre colour, and it was big, certainly more than big enough to house five business execs and their hangers-on.

I parked in the shade of a truly massive umbrella pine that was every inch as tall as the villa itself and which did a marvellous job of shading the area. Opening the door, I was assailed by an over-whelming aroma of jasmine in the air. In fact, the walls bordering the path appeared to be clothed in the off-white flowers and the sound of bees industriously buzzing from bloom to bloom filled the air. I was just climbing out when the ornately carved front door of the villa opened and a figure appeared.

This character's appearance came as a surprise but it perfectly suited the frosty welcome I had been given so far. Before coming here this morning, I had been expecting to meet a sober butler figure, maybe even one wearing a formal suit like something out of *Downton Abbey* but, instead, this guy looked more like a profes-sional wrestler. He was wearing tracksuit trousers and a T-shirt soaked in sweat, from which powerful, tattooed forearms emerged, ending in a pair of massive hands. He had shoulders like a bull and a completely shaved head. He was one of those people who don't have a neck. His head somehow just emerged from his shoulders without narrowing around the throat, like an upturned flowerpot. He hadn't shaved, and the black stubble around his jowls did little to sweeten his appearance. He took two or three steps towards me.

'You don't park here. This is for the guests only.' From the aggressive way he addressed me, it was clear that his mood hadn't improved since our brief conversation at the gatepost. Maybe he was grumpy by nature or maybe it was just because I'd interrupted him in the middle of a serious workout. Over my years as a police officer, I had met my fair share of hard guys, or at least guys who wanted to give the impression of being hard, so I plastered on a friendly smile.

'Of course, if you'd like to tell me where you want me to park, I'll move.'

I saw him hesitate while he checked me out. I was probably an inch or two taller than him and ten to fifteen years older than him and a lot less broad in the beam. I reckon I'm still pretty fit for my age but I had no illusions as to how I might fare in a stand-up fight with this guy. Okay, so I had boxed for the force back in the mists of time, but I had never come across an opponent like this in the ring. From the way his T-shirt bulged, he had muscles in places where I didn't even have places, so I just kept smiling. Finally, he appeared to come to a decision.

'Follow me.' He ran down the steps and began jogging around the front of the house towards the far left-hand side. I climbed back into the van and followed him as instructed, wondering idly how often he needed to buy new shorts as his bulging leg muscles meant that I could see the already stretched material on his inner thighs rubbing together as he ran. We skirted the side of the house and took another gravelled track that led away from the house towards a cluster of outbuildings less than a hundred yards further on. The man mountain stopped when he got there and indicated that I should park between an old well and a white Ducato van. I did as instructed, turned off the engine and climbed out. He was still doing his hard-man act but, when I opened the boot and Oscar jumped out, a remarkable sea change came over him. Oscar, always a friendly dog, trotted across to say hello to him and my guide instantly morphed from Tyson Fury into David Attenborough. He squatted down and started stroking Oscar, who gave him the full old-pals greeting complete with tail wagging so hard, the whole rear half of his body wagged with it. When the man straightened up again, he was smiling.

'That's a handsome dog you have there. He's a Labrador, isn't he?' He spoke Italian with a strong, but quite intelligible, Tuscan accent.

'That's right. He's only three so he's still a bit boisterous.' By this time, Oscar was standing up on his hind legs, pawing at the man for more attention.

'He's a very nice dog.' The man looked up at me again and held out his free hand. 'My name's Riccardo, but everybody calls me Rocky.'

We shook hands and I did my best to avoid wincing. 'I can see how you got your nickname. You must spend a lot of time working out.'

He nodded. 'Three hours every day if I can. It depends how much work there is here at the villa.' His expression had definitely softened by now. 'Sorry I was a bit abrupt before. You got me right at the end of a set of one-arm press-ups.'

'Good for you. These days, I don't think I could even do one of them.' I looked around as he continued to ruffle Oscar's ears. 'I was told that there would be accommodation for me in an apartment?'

'It's here, above the old stables. Come on up and I'll show you.'

Oscar and I followed him through a door and up a flight of wooden stairs. We emerged into a charming room with scrubbed floorboards, a stone fireplace and hefty, rough-hewn beams supporting the ceiling. There was a smart, modern kitchen area over to one side with a granite worktop and shiny, modern units, while in the other direction, there was a dining table and a pair of sofas. It was certainly a whole lot more luxurious than my own little house in the Florentine hills.

'There are two bedrooms through there.' He waved towards a door at the far end. 'Antonella has made up both rooms, so take your pick.'

'Antonella?'

'My wife. She does the housekeeping and I do the garden, grounds, odd jobs and generally keep an eye on the place for Gus.'

'And Gus is...?'

'The boss. Augustus Cornish, owner of Villa Gregory S.r.l.'

The name implied that Rocky's boss was a descendent of Lord Augustus Cornish who had bought the villa after the war. S.r.l. was the equivalent of Ltd in the UK. 'The villa is a limited company? I suppose it's a bit too big to be a private home, even for somebody with a lot of money.'

Rocky nodded. 'Gus rents the villa out by the day for weddings, meetings and local events or for longer periods for groups like the people arriving tomorrow.' I saw him study me a bit more closely. 'Are you Secret Service or something like that? You've got that sort of look about you.'

Coming from the muscleman, I took that as a compliment. 'I used to be in the UK police, but now I have a private investigation agency in Florence. I know hardly anything about the people who're coming this weekend. What about you? Have any of them been here before?'

'I only know the man who's arriving this evening, Mr Derby. The boss threw a Christmas party here last year and the house was full of big names from the world of politics, business and sport. We had an Olympic swimmer and a downhill ski champion as well as some of the richest people in Europe.' He grinned at me. 'Gus likes mixing with the rich and famous. He rented the villa to a couple of very well-known Hollywood actors last summer. I'm not allowed to tell you their names but they were real, global stars.'

I looked impressed and decided not to mention my recent encounter with megastar Selena Gardner. 'And what about Mr Cornish? You say he likes mixing with the guests – does that mean he lives here?'

'He has his own apartment on the top floor of the villa. He's in Rome at the moment but he told me he'll be back tomorrow.'

Rocky gave me the code to open the electric gates to the road so I could get in and out, and we exchanged phone numbers. Thanks to the intervention of my four-legged friend, his grumpy persona had disappeared, and he was now friendly and open. Underneath the intimidating façade, he was a nice guy. After chatting some more, mainly about the house itself and its history, he left me and returned to his arduous training regime. Rather him than me.

I got my stuff out of the van and emptied the contents of the cold box I had brought from home into the fridge in the apartment. I also brought in Oscar's basket and put it in front of the empty fireplace in the living room, but I had little doubt that I would find him sleeping beside my bed – if not on it – when I woke up next morning. Before going into the house to start doing my electronic sweep, I decided to check out the grounds and, in particular, the perimeter to see just how secure the estate was.

Oscar and I had a very pleasant stroll through the grounds of the villa. It was a huge area, probably the size of two football pitches. To the rear of the house was a broad terrace with steps down to a well-tended, ornamental garden with meticulously clipped box hedges and another magnificent stone fountain. Beyond that was an expanse of remarkably lush lawn that was damp underfoot. A number of powerful-looking sprinklers around the edges indicated how Rocky managed to keep it looking so lush, in spite of the near-drought conditions. At the far end of the lawn, there was another pristine hedge, behind which I spotted a swimming pool. Fortunately, there was a gate and it was closed or I knew that my water-obsessed Labrador would have been in there like a shot.

It soon became clear that the brick wall – almost three metres high – continued all the way around the estate, making a very

effective barrier against intruders. There was a dense mass of
shrubs and bushes against it, particularly at the far extreme of the
estate, so I resolved to take a walk around the outside as well to
double-check that there weren't any openings I hadn't been able to
spot. Assuming the wall was intact all the way around, this meant
that the only access was through the main gate, which would make
my job in assuring privacy even easier.

At the far south-eastern corner of the grounds, I found the
replica Leaning Tower that Anna had told me about. Trees had
grown up around it, effectively masking most of it from the villa, or
at least from the lower floors, but no doubt when it was first built,
there would have been no trees to spoil the view. It certainly was a
faithful replica, and it really did lean alarmingly, just as the real
tower used to do until considerable and costly work was under-
taken thirty years ago to stabilise it and reduce the angle of the
lean before it all came tumbling down.

It was easy to see that this replica had been built in a hurry and
on a budget. Instead of white marble, this tower was made of brick
and timber, and it had been rendered with plaster and painted
white so that from a distance, it could pass for the real thing to a
photographer back at the villa or a casual observer who couldn't
be bothered to take the five-minute walk down here. The pillars
and carvings of the original had been replaced by carved wood,
painted white like the walls, but even so, I wondered how long it
had taken and how much it had cost for a gang of builders to
construct it while the owner of the villa paced nervously up and
down, wondering if it was going to be convincing enough to save
him from losing face in front of his friends.

I've never climbed the real tower and I have absolutely no
desire to do so, but my fear of heights didn't stop me climbing this
one. Anna had said that it was a one-sixth replica and I estimated
that it was probably about ten metres high, about the height of the

roof of a three-storey house – and that's about as high as I feel comfortable to go. A low doorway had been installed on the far side of the tower, out of sight of the villa, and inside, it was completely bare except for a simple wooden staircase that led up to the top. It creaked a bit but felt solid enough and not only did *I* manage it, but so did Oscar. From the top, I could look over the perimeter wall, and in the direction of Pisa, I could immediately see the little hillock that had prevented the original owner of the villa from getting a view of the historic centre of the town. From my vantage point, I had no trouble spotting the real Leaning Tower and the huge bulk of the cathedral with the circular baptistery alongside it. In the distance, behind the city was the dark-green outline of the tree-clad foothills of the Apennines.

Looking back in the direction of the villa, I discovered that I could see it almost in its entirety over the tops of the surrounding trees. It was probably about two hundred metres away and I spotted a female figure meticulously brushing the tiled floor of the terrace in readiness for the new arrivals. Presumably, this was Rocky's wife, Antonella. From up here, I also had a good view around the estate and could make out my own apartment in the old stable block in one direction and the swimming pool in the other. It occurred to my suspicious mind that a sniper intent on committing murder couldn't really ask for a better position from which to fire. I sincerely hoped nothing like that was going to happen this week.

4

SUNDAY AFTERNOON

My sweep of the twenty-two rooms of the villa took all morning and some of the afternoon. I was accompanied much of the time by Rocky, who was clearly fascinated and impressed by the technology. I was less impressed. The detector I had bought came with some very good reviews and was allegedly being used by numerous law-enforcement agencies around the world, as well, no doubt, as a lot of less legitimate organisations. Unfortunately, as well as detecting microphones and cameras, it had an annoying habit of also reacting to power points, light switches and anything metal, which considerably lengthened the time it took me to check each room.

The rooms themselves were well-furnished in a mixture of styles and somebody, possibly the original owner, had clearly had a fascination with antique weaponry. In the main entrance hall, there were a couple of muskets and several ancient flintlock pistols on display. From the look of them, they were probably at least two hundred years old. In the music room – a fine room lined with bookshelves and with a magnificent grand piano in the middle – my scanner started screaming as I approached a crowded rack on the wall containing several dozen clearly very old daggers and short swords below a shield with a crest on it of what looked like three ravens and a tower. I went over and took a closer look at the knives, lifting several of them out and feeling the weight of what were very nasty weapons. I glanced across at the big man.

'Somebody could do a lot of damage with one of these.'

'You aren't kidding.'

I replaced the daggers carefully and continued with the sweep. Alongside these was a full suit of armour, polished until it shone. It looked great but, like the daggers, it drove my scanner crazy and it took me ages to be as certain as I could be that the room was bug free. I decided to advise Piers to try to avoid using the music room for any confidential discussions just in case. The villa emanated good taste and a sense of history, as well as an unmistakable atmosphere of considerable wealth. It was evident that the owners of this place over the years had certainly not been short of a bob or two.

It was three-thirty by the time I finished the sweep and went back to my apartment to feed myself and my ever-hungry dog. I sat down with a glass of cold water and let my mind dwell on my upcoming meeting with Anna's daughter. Anna had phoned Virginia earlier in the month to break the news to her that the person employed to look after security for the villa was going to be me. Virginia hadn't reacted well but had called her mum back a couple of days later to say that, although she still had no desire to meet me, she had thought it over and had decided not to ask to be replaced. Evidently, ambition had triumphed over emotion. She and her boss, Jonathan Farmer, would be arriving on Monday afternoon. My meeting with her promised to be an interesting encounter, and I glanced down at my dog.

'I'm counting on you to turn on the charm tomorrow, Oscar.

Virginia probably isn't going to like me, at least initially, but surely a big, soppy Labrador will be able to win her round.'

He briefly interrupted his post-prandial ablutions to look up at the sound of his name and I hoped he knew what he had to do. I tried to put myself in Virginia's position. Naturally, if she was still close to her father, she would find it hard to accept another man in her mother's life, but after so long, it seemed only fair to me to let her mum move on – but then it wasn't my mother we were talking about. I resolved to keep a low profile as far as Virginia was concerned and if we actually had to speak, I would make sure we kept it to business and nothing more.

Just after five, I got a text message from Rocky.

Mr Derby just arrived. Wants to see you.

I texted him back that I was on my way and set off for the villa with Oscar. I walked around to the rear of the villa and when I spotted two figures outside on the terrace, I made straight for them.

Malcolm Derby looked as if he was in his early fifties. The perfectly ironed, light-blue linen shirt he was wearing was very smart, and no doubt expensive, and he exuded an air of bonhomie. He wouldn't have looked out of place compering one of those 'buy yourself a holiday home on the Costa del Sol' programmes, although I wondered whether the dark rings under his eyes had been caused by pressure of work or something else. Mind you, even though his eyes looked weary, I knew that with my greying hair and my latest batch of wrinkles, I looked a whole lot worse, although I was probably only a year or two older than he was. Maybe I should have listened to my ex-wife when she had been banging on about moisturiser years ago.

Malcolm Derby smiled when he saw me – which was promising.

'Chief Inspector Armstrong, good to see you.'

He gave me a firm handshake, which fortunately was quite a lot lower down on the Richter scale than the crunching handshake I had received from Rocky. Piers Cooper-Stevenson, still clad all in black, remained a deferential distance behind his employer so I just gave him a nod and produced an answering smile for Mr Derby.

'And to see you too, Mr Derby. And it's just Dan Armstrong these days, no police rank any more.'

To my surprise, he went on to reveal that he knew a whole lot more about me than I had expected. 'You come highly recommended and it would appear that you're a man of many talents. I happened upon an interesting article about you and your literary career in *The Sunday Times* a month or two ago. I believe congratulations are in order. Your book's doing very well, I believe.'

'Thank you, I can still hardly believe it myself. Fingers crossed.'

The first of my murder mysteries set here in Tuscany had been published earlier this year and, with the help of a great publisher and a very flattering article from a journalist friend, it was achieving a lot more success than I could have hoped for. But I knew I wasn't being paid to talk about my writing, so I quickly returned to the matter in hand. 'I've done a complete sweep of the villa and I'm as certain as I can be that there's no electronic surveillance going on. No audio and no cameras, so you should be completely safe – although the music room with all its metal ornaments should probably be avoided just in case. As I told Mr Cooper-Stevenson, I'd like to do a sweep of the main rooms once a day to be on the safe side. Will you be following a regular schedule? When could I gain access each day without disturbing anybody?'

'I'll have to talk it through with the others tomorrow night when everybody's here, but I would imagine that we'll try to sit down together at least once a day, probably in the mornings. Of course, it's only fair that we should all get a bit of time off to take advantage of the beautiful weather and to visit this historic city, so I would imagine most afternoons will see people out and about, doing the tourist thing. Provisionally, why don't you plan on carrying out your checks in the afternoons when you should have the place to yourself?'

'That's fine. I'll wait for you to give me definite confirmation tomorrow. I've taken a look around outside in the grounds and it all appears secure as far as anybody trying to come in to spy on you is concerned, but I'll take Oscar for a walk in a moment and inspect the perimeter walls from the outside, just to be sure that there aren't any obvious places where one of your rivals or an enthusiastic journalist could gain access.'

He nodded a couple of times. 'Excellent, Mr Armstrong, that sounds fine. I'm afraid Piers and I are going to be busy now but maybe you'd like to join me for an aperitif this evening, say around seven? I'm taking my wife out for dinner later but it would be good to chat before then. You can tell me all about how you're finding life over here in Italy.' He looked around the gardens in silent appreciation for a few seconds. 'I admire your choice. Tuscany's a wonderful part of the world.'

I had been struggling with a vague sense of familiarity and it suddenly came to me. Malcolm Derby reminded me very much of the guy who had sold me a new car just a couple of years before my wife and I had divorced. I wondered idly if she still had it. Anyway, that man had emanated the same affable air as Derby and he had been trying – and succeeding – to sell me something. The suspicion dawned on me that I was almost certainly in the presence of a salesman – but of something a whole lot more expensive than a Ford Focus.

At that moment, I suddenly saw Oscar swivel his head towards the open French windows behind us and the end of his tail started wagging. A broad canine smile appeared on his face as a woman appeared at the door. As he trotted over to greet her, I took a close look at her. She was very attractive, probably still in her mid-thirties, and as she reached down to stroke Oscar's head, I couldn't miss a gold wedding ring and an engagement ring with a hefty diamond on it on her left hand.

'Come and meet our security chief, darling.'

Mr Derby gave her a beaming smile but, call me a suspicious old copper, I had a feeling he was trying just a little bit too hard. As confirmation of this impression, the look his wife gave him in return was definitely far from loving. Yes, she smiled, but I'm sure even Oscar could see it was a struggle for her. Interestingly, as she came towards us, I noticed two little red spots appear on the cheeks of Piers. I had a feeling that my Labrador wasn't the only one around here who liked this woman. Might this lead to trouble in paradise? I wondered.

'Mr Armstrong, I'd like you to meet my wife, Melanie. Melanie, darling, this is Dan Armstrong, formerly DCI Armstrong of the Metropolitan Police. Now he has the great good fortune to live here in Tuscany.'

Melanie Derby came across to offer me her hand.

'I'm pleased to meet you, Mr Armstrong.'

Her voice was low and her accent educated middle England. Close up, I could see that she was probably all of fifteen or even twenty years younger than her husband and the dark rings under her eyes, mirroring his own, made me wonder how their marriage was faring, but, I reminded myself, that wasn't my business. We exchanged a few pleasantries about how lovely the weather, Tuscany and my dog were, and then I took my leave so I could go and check the surrounding wall to be absolutely sure that there were no openings that I hadn't spotted.

Oscar and I walked back to the main gate and I punched the code Rocky had given me into the stainless-steel keypad set into the door pillar. Sure enough, the yellow light started flashing and the gates swung back towards me. I went out and waited until the gates had closed behind me before turning right and walking along the road for a couple of hundred yards until I reached the edge of the estate where the brick wall did a right-angle bend. There was a farm track here that allowed me to follow the line of the wall for several hundred metres to the far corner, inside which I knew the mini tower to be located, although the high wall and the overhanging greenery effectively screened it from view. As I walked, I picked up sticks to throw for Oscar to retrieve and while playing our game of fetch, I checked the wall for any openings or weaknesses. As far as I could see, it was all in good repair and would present a formidable obstacle to anybody hoping to get over it.

When I turned the corner so as to walk along the rear of the estate, I found that this involved skirting around the edge of a field planted with some sort of cereal, already waist-high. It was fortunate that the ground was so dry because I could see deep impressions in the soil beneath my feet where tractor tyres had dug into waterlogged ground in the past but, the way things were at the moment, water was in short supply and the earth was rock-hard. I kept an eye open for snakes, partly because I've never been a reptile fan, but mainly because I'd read that there were poisonous vipers in the nearby country park and the last thing I wanted was for Oscar or me to get bitten. Fortunately, all I saw were a few lizards who were clearly far more afraid of me than I was of them. They say the same thing about snakes, but I've never been convinced, so I tend to steer clear of them wherever possible.

Halfway along, I found an opening in the brick wall. It was a low arched doorway with a sturdy, wooden gate set into it. I gave it a push with my shoulder and turned the old iron ring handle in both directions but it didn't budge. As far as I could estimate, this lay directly behind the thickest of the bushes I had spotted earlier on the inside. No way in here either. I carried on following the wall until I emerged back onto the road again and returned to the main gates feeling confident that it would take a very determined and athletic journalist, paparazzo or industrial-espionage agent to get in.

At seven o'clock, as instructed, I went over to the villa and found Piers Cooper-Stevenson out on the terrace clad, as always, in black. After a hot day, it was still a very warm evening and I was just in shirtsleeves. Presumably, he had a different body thermostat from mine. Oscar had already worked out for himself that Piers wasn't a Labrador fan, so he ignored him and headed for the nearest patch of shade where he slumped down on the marble tiles. Seconds later, however, he jumped to his feet and headed for the French windows, tail wagging, as Antonella, Rocky's wife, appeared at the door.

'Good evening, gentlemen, can I get you a drink?' She spoke good English with a strong Tuscan accent. She was the complete antithesis of her musclebound husband: small, dainty and petite. 'And can I get your lovely dog anything?' Oscar looked up at her and wagged his tail hopefully. If he could have miraculously gained the power of speech, I have little doubt that he would have ordered a chateaubriand with a side order of sausages.

Clearly on his best behaviour, Piers let me choose first. I asked for a cold beer and, no doubt much to the chagrin of my dog, I told her Oscar didn't need anything. Piers settled for a glass of mineral water. After Antonella had gone off to get our drinks, I turned back to Piers and made an attempt at conversation. 'Have you been to Pisa before?' I saw him shake his head. 'It's a beautiful historic city. Hopefully, you'll get a bit of time off to go and see the sights. You can't come to Pisa without seeing the Leaning Tower, but the duomo is even more spectacular.'

He smiled nervously, glancing over my shoulder to check that his boss hadn't appeared. 'That would be nice, but it depends if I can take the time off. Apart from the meetings this week, I've brought a load of work with me.'

'Does Mr Derby keep you very busy?'

He nodded. 'You wouldn't believe how much we've got on at the moment. Like I told you, it's a very new company and we're working hard to build it up. And now, with this new venture, the workload has tripled.' He didn't go into detail about the new venture and I didn't ask.

'How long have you worked for Mr Derby?'

'I only started last autumn, so it's been quite a sharp learning curve.' He produced a little smile. 'I was at the BBC before and let's just say that they didn't keep me anything like as busy.'

I gave him a wink. 'But it's all valuable experience, I'm sure, for when you take over from Mr Derby as CEO of the company. Is that the plan?'

He gave me another little smile in return and I caught a fleeting glimpse of the ambitious young man beneath the façade. 'Something like that, if all goes well, but I've got a long way to go.'

'Tell me, what's Mr Derby like to work for? He looks a bit stressed to me.'

After another check over his shoulder, he answered. 'A *bit* stressed? He's been about two foot off the ground over the last couple of months in the build-up to this new project.' He lowered his voice. 'There's a lot riding on this week's meetings.'

Any further discussion of the subject was interrupted by the arrival of Antonella with our drinks, closely followed by Malcolm Derby himself, accompanied by his wife. They were both clutching glasses of sparkling wine. In a place like this, it wouldn't have surprised me to find that it was vintage champagne.

He came over to me and smiled genially before turning and issuing a brief instruction to Piers. 'I'm expecting an email any time now from AG. Keep a lookout for it and text me when it arrives.' He turned back to me and indicated his wife, who was stroking Oscar, who looked as though he was in rapture – he's always had a thing for the ladies. 'I thought you might be interested to know that you have a fan, Mr Armstrong. Melanie has read your book and she tells me it's excellent. Isn't that so, darling?'

His wife looked up and for the first time, I saw real animation on her face. 'I'm afraid I didn't put two and two together when Malcolm introduced us earlier. So you're Dan Armstrong, the author. How wonderful. I read *Death Amid the Vines* last month and thoroughly enjoyed it. If I'd known you were going to be here, I would have brought my copy with me for you to sign.'

I was genuinely amazed. 'That's wonderful to hear, thank you. It's the first book I've ever had published and you're just about the first person I've ever met who's admitted to having read my work. I'm delighted you enjoyed it.'

I spent an unexpectedly pleasant half-hour chatting to Mr and Mrs Derby. From time to time, Piers even put in a word or two, normally addressed to Mrs Derby, but I could see that his role as lackey demanded that he keep to the background. Although Mr Derby continued to play the perfect host – even though he was in fact my employer – my original impression that things were not exactly going swimmingly between him and his wife was reinforced during the course of the evening. She didn't exactly look unhappy, she just looked... I found myself searching for the word and finally it came to me: resigned. She looked resigned to her fate. I was sure that to many impartial observers the fate of being married to a rich man and living a lifestyle like this would have been enviable, but obviously, beneath the glitz and glamour, things weren't running quite as smoothly as she would have hoped. Still, I told myself not for the first time, this was their problem, not mine.

When they went off to sample the bright lights of Pisa – without Piers – I returned to my apartment to make myself an omelette. I'm sure it's a sign that I'm getting old, but I was more than happy at the prospect of a quiet night in.

5

MONDAY EARLY EVENING

By six o'clock the following evening, all the guests had arrived. I learned this from Piers, who came over to my apartment to tell me that I was invited to join the group for drinks at seven. After that, dinner would be taken outside on the terrace and then the main players might be disappearing into a private room for preliminary talks. Possibly under pressure from Mrs Derby, who had appeared remarkably interested in my nascent writing career, Piers informed me that I had been invited to join them not only for drinks but also for dinner – along with Oscar.

I had spent the day rechecking the main rooms for any unwanted snooping devices and had once more been able to give the place a clean bill of health. Oscar and I had also done another circuit of the perimeter, this time inside the grounds, and by struggling along a vestigial path through the shrubbery at the far end, I'd managed to ascertain that the little door in the end wall was firmly secured with two massive, old bolts, each well over a foot long.

I had just finished changing before going over to the villa when I got a call from Anna back in Florence.

'She's arrived.'

There was no need to ask to whom Anna was referring. I told her that I'd be meeting Virginia in just a matter of minutes and I queried what sort of mood she was in.

'She sounded stressed, but that's probably as a result of the journey. They flew over in Jonathan Farmer's private jet, but their departure was delayed by almost an hour and he was apparently getting very stroppy with all and sundry.'

'Well, all the more reason for me to go through with my plan of merging into the background and staying out of her way... and out of his way as well, for that matter.'

I went on to tell her that I had been invited to dine with the delegates, their wives and girlfriends – and quite possibly boyfriends. I had no idea of the identity of the other participants or indeed their gender – although I had a feeling most of the movers and shakers would be male. My limited experience of the world of high finance had told me that it was still pretty much a boys' club. I tried to make my voice as reassuring as possible.

'I'll make sure I sit at the opposite end of the table.'

Anna was still sounding apprehensive. 'Although she's been trying to sound disinterested, I got the feeling she's quite nervous at the thought of meeting you, so if the two of you do talk, try to tread softly.'

'She's not the only one who's nervous. I'm counting on Oscar to do the spade work. You know him; he's far better at turning on the charm than I am.'

Even so, I had to admit that I was feeling tense as I walked across to meet the woman who might even end up as my step-daughter one day. There was already a little group of people standing on the terrace dressed to the nines and clutching glasses of fizz. Two of the women were in long dresses and at least one man was wearing a tuxedo, and I was glad I had showered and changed into slightly more formal clothes before coming over. All right, I was only the hired help, but I felt it only right to do my best not to let the side down. I took up station not far from Piers – as ever all in black – over to one side of the terrace, told Oscar to sit down alongside me, and took a good look around. As I did so, I heard my name and saw a man I didn't immediately recognise approaching with a tray of drinks. It was Rocky, and this time he had morphed from professional wrestler to high-class, West End nightclub bouncer. He was squeezed into a tux that was struggling to contain the muscles within, and his bow tie clearly couldn't work out exactly where his neck started and finished.

'*Ciao*, Rocky, you're looking very smart.'

He grinned. 'The boss wants to put on a bit of a show for the big nobs.' He used the Italian expression *pezzi grossi* that literally translates as 'big pieces'.

'Augustus Cornish has returned, has he?'

He nodded. 'Didn't you see the Ferrari outside? He's in the kitchen with Antonella and the chef, doing a bit of peace-making.' He gave me a wink. 'This chef's new to us. Gus has flown him over from England specially for the week. He's supposed to be a celebrity chef – why would you want a chef from *England* over here? – and he's behaving like a prima donna. If he carries on, Antonella's told me she'll clout him with a pan.'

I was reminded of Virgilio's story of the bus driver clonked over the head and pushed to his death by his wife and I sincerely hoped the kitchen situation here wouldn't escalate to that degree. I helped myself to a glass of champagne and Rocky continued on his rounds while I returned to studying the people around me.

I recognised one of the faces instantly. Eleanor Leonard was a stunningly beautiful woman, probably not yet thirty, with smooth, black skin and a mass of hair cascading to her shoulders. In spite of her youth, she was one of the most famous opera singers in the world, with a glittering career behind her that had seen her perform to packed houses everywhere from La Scala to Carnegie Hall and often in front of royalty and heads of state. She had recently married a famous, if reclusive, Greek shipping magnate called Aristotelis, who was at least twice her age, and her face had been all over the papers and on TV. I whistled quietly to myself. The UK's youngest billionaire and now a massive international celebrity: it looked as though the participants in this week's meeting were drawn from the highest level.

Alongside Ms Leonard were two men and a woman. I didn't recognise any of the three so I queried this with Piers – keeping my voice down. He was only too happy to fill me in.

'The guy with the grey hair and the dark tux is Erich Baumgartner. He works out of Zurich and he and his wife head up a financial management company whose registered office is in Liechtenstein.' He raised his eyebrows. 'One of the biggest hedge-fund companies in the world. That's his wife beside him.'

Mr Baumgartner looked as though he was in his sixties, but his wife could have been any age from thirty to eighty, with suspiciously golden hair. The skin of her face was so taut, I was reminded of the description I had once heard of an ageing Hollywood starlet who had allegedly had so many nips and tucks that when she winked, her left leg lifted. I know very little about women's fashion – or men's, for that matter – but even I could see that her long evening dress, sparkling diamond necklace and satin gloves that reached up above her elbows – although a bit OTT even for this illustrious company – hadn't come cheap.

'What about the other guy? The one with the pink tux and the D'Artagnan beard?'

'Antoine Dujardin, French Canadian. They say he owns the rights to half of all undersea oil deposits in the Arctic Circle.'

'Did he come with a wife or partner?'

'I'm not totally sure. Maybe.'

'You're going to have to explain.'

Piers grimaced. 'Dujardin arrived with a... lady.' He took his time choosing the word. 'She's booked in as his PA, but I have a feeling she might do a bit more than that for him.'

I looked around but couldn't see another woman. 'And where is she now?'

A hint of a smile crossed his face. 'I would guess in her boudoir, but you'll recognise her when she appears.' He lowered his voice and whispered like a guilty schoolboy, 'I think "unforgettable" would be a fair way of describing her.'

At that moment, another couple appeared at the French doors. He was maybe in his mid or late thirties and he had evidently eschewed dressing up. He was simply wearing jeans and a white cotton shirt. When I say 'simply', there was still the minor matter of a thirty-thousand-pound Rolex Submariner watch on his arm, just so nobody could confuse Jonathan Farmer with an ordinary member of the great unwashed. He was a good-looking man with close-cropped, blond hair and a tanned face. He looked as if he kept himself fit – but not to the same extreme extent as Rocky here at the villa. Alongside him was a young woman and I recognised her instantly even though this was the first time I had ever seen her. It had to be Virginia. The resemblance to her mother was unmistakable. With her long legs, glossy, dark hair and her high cheekbones, she was the spitting image of her mum.

What was interesting was the almost palpable tremor that spread around the others out here on the terrace when Farmer appeared. It was hard to put my finger on, but I felt sure I could detect surprise, apprehension and also a considerable degree of antipathy. In particular, I saw a frown appear on the Canadian's face, while the Swiss lady turned sharply away and started surveying the gardens of the villa as intently as if she were intending putting in an offer to buy it. Eleanor Leonard suddenly developed a fascination with her shoes and dropped her eyes to the floor and even Melanie Derby looked away, although her husband hurried across to greet the newcomer. Evidently, Jonathan Farmer's reputation had preceded him.

Before coming here, I had checked him out on the Internet and had found it peppered with anecdotes of his eccentric behaviour. There was no question that he was a brilliant – and ruthless – businessman with a nose for a lucrative deal, and not too many scruples about how he made his money. According to what I'd read, in his private life he was also far from mundane. On one occasion, he'd climbed the outside of his high-rise office block in central London without ropes and in midwinter had been photographed swimming naked off the coast of Aberdeen, of all places. While this and other escapades like skydiving, bungee jumping and seven-day drunken binges spoke volumes about his stamina, it didn't quite chime with his role as financial genius. Along with his alleged addiction to beautiful women, fast cars and hallucinatory substances, it was clear that he sometimes struggled to inspire confidence in more staid investors, and rumours of dodgy deals abounded. What, I wondered, might he be up to here in Pisa and how might he go down with the other participants? From their reaction to his appearance, it didn't bode well.

My musings were interrupted by a voice from behind me.

'Mr Armstrong, I presume. Do, please, introduce me to your companion.'

I turned to find myself face to face with a suntanned man, maybe in his forties, wearing an immaculate blue blazer and white slacks. He looked as if he'd just stepped off the bridge of the *Titanic*. A pair of sunglasses on his head held his perfectly styled hair in place and I had little doubt that I was looking at the owner of Villa Gregory.

'Mr Cornish? I'm very pleased to meet you. I'm Dan and this is Oscar.'

He leant forward and ruffled Oscar's ears. 'Hello, Oscar, what a handsome chap you are. We always had Labs in the family when I was growing up. I'd love to have another one, but I travel around so much these days, it wouldn't really be fair on the poor thing.' He straightened up and looked at me. 'Malcolm tells me you used to be a senior officer in the Metropolitan police. What made you decide to settle down in Tuscany?'

I gave him the usual answer about the climate, the history, the food and drink and the Tuscan people, but I didn't mention Anna. Instinctively, as I thought of her, I shot a look sideways at Virginia and, just as I did so, she happened to glance in my direction and, for a moment, our eyes met. She must have spotted something in my expression and as recognition dawned, she instantly and ostentatiously swung her head away from me. I gave a mental shrug. I hadn't really been expecting anything else. I returned my attention to the owner of the villa, whose eyes were now trained on Jonathan Farmer.

'You have some illustrious company here this week, Mr Cornish.'

'Not so much illustrious as infamous.' His voice was studiously low and his eyes remained firmly fixed on Virginia's boss. I gave him a gentle prompt.

'Jonathan Farmer?'

He shot me a conspiratorial glance. 'He's the top of the heap, but he's not the only one. Malcolm certainly can pick them!' Realising that he was probably speaking out of turn, he gave me a little smile. 'But what do I know, eh? I'm just the innkeeper.' I thought I could detect a hint of bitterness in his tone, but seconds later, his whole demeanour changed. 'Ah… do excuse me, Mr Armstrong.'

His head had turned towards the French windows as a woman

emerged. And not just any woman. This one probably wasn't much older than Virginia, maximum thirty, and with her mass of blonde hair, she was very definitely unmissable although, being a suspicious detective, I wondered if it had started life that colour. She had a pair of cherry-red lips that had been injected with so much filler that you could probably have stuck her onto a window pane and left her there, and so much eye shadow, she resembled a panda. She was wearing a near-transparent, light-pink dress with what would be referred to euphemistically as a 'daring' neckline, and even from five metres away, I was hit by a tsunami of perfume. For a fraction of a second, I caught Piers' eye. He had been right about 'unforgettable'. There could be no doubt about it. This lady had to be Antoine Dujardin's PA – if that really was her actual function. To confirm my suspicions, she clip-clopped across the marble to the Canadian on her six-inch heels and gave him an affectionate smile. He turned towards her and smiled back – to my cynical eye, maybe a bit less affectionately.

I noticed that Oscar's eyes had followed her all the way and he glanced up at me as much as to say, *Would you just look at that!*

I reached down and touched his head. 'It's rude to stare, dog.'

Augustus Cornish was already heading across to join the little group and he was soon expertly schmoozing the new arrival. I allowed my eyes to rest for a moment on Mr Dujardin's face and found him looking surprisingly unaffected. Maybe she really was just his PA after all and, at the end of the day, how she chose to look was her affair and hers alone. I was giving myself a mental telling-off for judging by appearances when I noticed that Dujardin was far more interested in studying Jonathan Farmer. I felt sure I could see displeasure lurking just beneath his apparently impassive features as he stared at Farmer with thinly veiled dislike. And he wasn't the only one; I was interested to see that few, if any, of the other guests had offered to shake hands with him and

Farmer was standing apart from the group, talking to Virginia. For whatever reason, he certainly appeared to be shunned by most.

Back in my office in Florence, Piers had told me that the meeting would consist of four main players plus his boss. I did a quick count-up of who was here: Antoine Dujardin, Erich Baumgartner and his wife, who presumably together counted as one player, Eleanor Leonard and Jonathan Farmer. That made the four and, right on cue, the host of the meeting appeared at the door with his wife. Malcolm Derby was wearing a midnight-blue dinner jacket and Melanie Derby was looking particularly lovely tonight in an elegant, if conservative, long, light-grey dress. Unlike Frau Baumgartner, she was wearing no jewellery or evening gloves and unlike Dujardin's PA, she had little or no make-up. As her eyes alighted on me – or more probably on Oscar – she gave a little smile. I smiled back and Oscar wagged his tail.

Assuming that Eleanor Leonard's reclusive husband hadn't left his hideaway on his private island in the Peloponnese, it looked as though the gathering was complete: the *pezzi grossi*, Malcolm Derby and his wife, two assistants and whatever the blonde bombshell was. I took another good look at Virginia while she was standing chatting with Jonathan Farmer and I couldn't miss the way her boss had a habit of laying an affectionate hand on her arm every time he made a point. My suspicions as to his true intentions in bringing her here resurfaced and I wondered how that was going to pan out if I was right.

The sound of somebody striking a glass with a coin or a key attracted my attention and the attention of everybody on the terrace, including Oscar. It was Malcolm Derby.

'Ladies and gentlemen, a warm welcome to the lovely Villa Gregory.' He waved in the direction of Augustus Cornish. 'My thanks to my good friend, Gus, for letting us hold our meetings here. I hope our negotiations this week will result in the creation of something amazing. I look forward to answering all your questions about this exciting project and we're going to have a video call from Mr Grunstock himself at ten o'clock tomorrow morning so you can hear direct from him what we're planning. He has asked me to give you his apologies but he's involved in a high-level meeting in South Africa at the moment. If all goes well, he will try to drop in to see us later in the week. Tonight is just all about eating well and relaxing. Thank you for coming and I hope that this proves to be an interesting and profitable week for us all.'

Although I was being paid handsomely for my time, I had a feeling that this week would prove considerably more profitable for the *pezzi grossi*.

6

MONDAY EVENING

Dinner on the terrace was interesting. The food was excellent, although anybody who had come here expecting an Italian meal would have been surprised and disappointed. I discovered in the course of the evening that the chef in question, although parachuted in from London, was in fact French, and that the evening's cuisine was going to be all French. However, from my point of view, the food took second place to the person seated across the table from me.

I had deliberately chosen what I thought to be a safe seat at one end of the table, with Melanie Derby alongside me, but Jonathan Farmer had then elected to plonk himself down beside Antoine Dujardin's colourful assistant, right opposite Melanie, with Virginia obediently taking up station on his other side. This meant that Anna's daughter ended up barely three feet directly opposite me. Every time I looked up, she was there and, of course, she had the same problem. Unfortunately, my plan of using Oscar as a peace ambassador had been thwarted by a divider running along beneath the centre of the table that prevented me from sending him across to give her the full big-brown-eye treatment.

She studiously ignored me, and I did my best to do the same. Fortunately, much of my attention was taken up in conversation with Melanie, who kept on returning to the subject of my writing. She was looking particularly stressed this evening and I wondered if this was because of something her husband had said or done or whether she had a problem with one of the guests. I didn't have time to speculate as talk of my writing attracted the attention of one or two other people at the table and I soon found myself in the embarrassing position of having to answer questions about what was for me still a very new occupation. I gradually managed to steer the conversation away from myself and as the evening progressed and the sun dropped towards the horizon, I was able to check out the others, starting with Virginia's boss.

Jonathan Farmer was one of those people who just can't sit still for a second. His eyes were constantly jumping from person to person and, call me suspicious, but I felt I'd seen that same overexcited gleam in the eyes of people who had been snorting something they shouldn't have. Maybe I was wrong, but he definitely looked and sounded hyper. He was outspoken and clearly very bright and knowledgeable about everything from computer programming to Michelangelo, and there could be no doubt that he thought he was the best thing since sliced bread. Alongside him, Virginia spent a lot of her time watching him as well, and when her attention was directed at her boss, I took a closer look at her, trying to analyse her reaction to him. As well as being a very attractive woman, she was also obviously intelligent, and I heard her contribute a lot of facts about Tuscany and its history to the conversation, and when she spoke Italian to Rocky or Antonella, she sounded like a native.

As far as I could see from her closely guarded expression, she clearly admired Farmer but, equally clearly, she was doing her best to ignore or rebuff his advances. These took the form of regular touches to her bare arm or hands, knowing looks, and the sorts of comments that any sensible boss doesn't start levelling at his female staff unless he wants to find himself at the wrong end of an industrial tribunal. Of course, a good-looking man in his position with all his money probably wasn't used to women turning him down. To my mind, there could be no doubt that Farmer fancied Virginia, although he also spent a lot of time pawing the Canadian woman on his other side. I was unable to tell whether this was to the disapproval – or more – of Antoine Dujardin, who was sitting a bit further along on my side of the table and so invisible to me.

From the amount of wine he was consuming, I wondered whether Farmer was trying to build up a bit of Dutch courage before launching an assault on one of the women, and I reckoned Virginia would do well to lock her bedroom door tonight. How all that alcohol would mix with the white powder I suspected him of taking remained to be seen.

I definitely got the impression that she was turning him down, albeit as discreetly and diplomatically as possible, but maybe that was just wishful thinking on my part. In my thirty years in the murder squad, I'd seen a lot of things, but rich men hooking up with beautiful young women, treating them well, marrying them and then both living happily ever after had unfortunately only too often ended in heartache for the women, and I didn't want that to happen to my girlfriend's daughter. Whatever she might think of me, I found that I was harbouring almost paternal feelings towards her and developing what was probably an unfair dislike of this man, Jonathan Farmer, who had, after all, done me no harm.

As Melanie sporadically addressed random comments to me about the weather, the gardens or Oscar, I checked out the other people around the table. Frau Baumgartner said very little, ate very little, and I don't think I saw her smile once. Whether this was because her skin was pulled so tight, she was physically incapable of moving the appropriate face muscles or whether she just wasn't in the mood was uncertain, but my money would have been on a combination of both. On the other hand, I was mildly surprised to find that her husband at the far end of the table, in spite of his formal appearance, was the life and soul of the party, telling some very risqué jokes and recounting a fascinating and probably highly slanderous series of anecdotes involving world leaders he had met. Like Jonathan Farmer, he was also indulging liberally in alcohol and his cheeks were getting redder and redder. This was the first time I'd met a Swiss financier and he certainly didn't fit the stereotype of a gnome from Zurich I had imagined.

Eleanor Leonard, the soprano, said very little but she appeared to be enjoying the Swiss gentleman's stories, as did Malcolm Derby. He was also sitting on my side of the table so I couldn't see his face but I could hear that he was playing the role of cordial host very well and positively oozing charm. Next to him was Antoine Dujardin, who hardly said a word. When I did hear him speak, it was with no trace of a French accent although Piers told me he was from Quebec.

As for his flashy lady friend, I wasn't sure what I'd been expecting from her, but it wouldn't have surprised me if she'd turned out to have a voice like a foghorn and a stock of even steamier stories than Erich Baumgartner. Instead, she spoke very little and appeared to absorb the attentions of Jonathan Farmer beside her, smiling politely at his jokes, but without any real conviction. She didn't draw back from his quite blatant advances, but I definitely got the impression she wasn't feeling very comfortable next to him and I couldn't blame her for that. From my position, I was unable to see her boss's facial expressions but I couldn't shift an ungenerous hunch that there might well be a considerable degree of overlap between her professional and her personal functions. Like it or lump it, first impressions count, and my first impression of this lady had not immediately been one of an efficient co-worker. My ex-wife had often accused me of jumping to conclusions about people so I made a concerted effort to suspend my disbelief. Maybe I *was* just a cynical old copper as she had so often said.

After an exquisite dish of lobster meat and avocado salad surrounded by half a dozen oysters as hors d'oeuvres, we moved on to cheese and cauliflower soufflés, and I couldn't fault either. However bizarre it might seem to have brought a French chef from England to a villa in Italy, the results were spectacular and, from the look of the empty plates around me, my view appeared to be shared by most of my fellow diners – with the possible exception of Frau Baumgartner and Melanie, who appeared to have little appetite. Heartfelt lugubrious sighs from under the table indicated that Oscar felt he was being unfairly excluded but, as it turned out, he was to get his treat in the end. The main course was roast lamb and Antonella whispered in my ear that she'd asked the chef to let me have the bone for my four-legged friend.

I was pleased to see that at least the red wine was Italian – some excellent Barolo – while the white was an equally good Burgundy. Across the table from me, Jonathan Farmer was still putting the booze away at pace and the lustre in his eyes had been replaced by a more glazed look. I wondered how level-headed he was likely to be by the end of the meal and reflected that it was just as well the meetings proper wouldn't start until the next day. The good news from Virginia's point of view was that he was now doing less groping and, indeed, was looking quite subdued.

By the time we had all finished our *tarte aux fraises* with meringue ice cream and rich, dark-chocolate sauce, I reckoned I'd pretty well worked out the dynamic of the week's meetings. As far as I could see, Malcolm Derby was selling and the others were buying – or at least that was what he was hoping would happen.

Although few details of the proposed new venture were aired out here in public, it was clear that he was expecting the *pezzi grossi* to dig deep to finance a massive media project on a global scale. By the sound of it, the returns could prove to be enormous, but I had a feeling the risks might be of similar dimensions. Well, I told myself, that wasn't my problem. I was more than happy to leave that to the billionaires.

At just before ten, we were all invited to get up and go inside the villa to one of the large and luxurious lounges where coffee – and peppermint tea for Frau Baumgartner – was served. Almost immediately, the main players, shadowed by Piers, collected together in a conspiratorial huddle at one end of the room. Jonathan Farmer was swaying a bit and looked a little unsteady on his feet, which came as no surprise, and I was interested to see that Frau Baumgartner stayed close to the side of her husband – who wasn't looking too steady either. This left me at the other end of the room with only four other people: Augustus Cornish, Antoine Dujardin's companion, whose name I now discovered to be Eugenie, Virginia and Melanie Derby, who immediately excused herself and disappeared off to bed. Gus Cornish was all over Eugenie in a mixture of English, Italian and French, although she didn't appear to reciprocate his advances. In fact, she sounded remarkably balanced. It was looking increasingly as though I *had* been guilty of jumping to conclusions about her, based solely on her appearance.

As for Virginia, she was still avoiding even looking at me so I helped myself to a quick espresso and took my leave, explaining that Oscar needed a walk. When I went out onto the terrace again, I found Rocky waiting for me with a heavy bag containing what looked like half a sheep in it and Oscar's eyes lit up. I took the bag, asked Rocky to thank Antonella and the chef, and headed for home, closely followed by my dog, nostrils flared.

After depositing the lamb leftovers just inside the door of my apartment, I went out into the grounds for Oscar's evening promenade. This developed into quite a long walk as I took the opportunity of doing a complete tour of the perimeter at the same time, double-checking that all was still as it ought to be. While Oscar did his best to mark almost every tree we came across, I looked back from time to time at the villa. All lights were blazing on the ground floor while upstairs, I could see lights in only two rooms and I wondered idly if one of these belonged to Virginia. I hoped once again that she would lock her door in case her boss decided to become amorous.

It was a wonderful, clear night and the stars were already twinkling high above us. The path through the grounds was made of white gravel and Oscar's dark shape stood out clearly against it as he trotted ahead of me. I breathed deeply, savouring the warm evening and my brief exposure to the high life. The villa and its extensive grounds were a delight and the atmosphere out here under the trees, surrounded by the little yellow pinpricks of light of the fireflies, was positively romantic. The Mancunian industrialist who had built this place had certainly known what he was doing. I hoped very much that Anna would be able to come and sample it, if only for a few hours, later this week. Whether I would be on speaking terms with her daughter by then remained to be seen.

Oscar and I did a full circle and ended up at the far corner by the replica Leaning Tower. I stopped for a seat on a convenient bench and thought about phoning Anna with a progress report. On reflection, I decided to let it wait until the next day, by which time I might have something more positive to tell her than that her daughter had totally ignored me. On the way back, I saw the glow of lights as we neared the pool and I heard splashing and voices as some of the guests were having a late-night swim. After a huge meal and a lot of alcohol, I hoped whoever they were would be careful. It didn't sound like a very clever idea to me. I wondered who they might be but decided not to investigate for fear of giving Oscar the chance to plunge into the water. Even if Gus Cornish didn't object to Labrador hair in his nice, clean pool, I didn't relish the idea of sharing my bedroom with a damp dog.

When we returned to the flat, I made Oscar's day by giving him a bowlful of meat but decided to save the bone until the morning. I knew from experience that if I were to give it to him now, I wouldn't get a wink of sleep because of the ominous cracking and crunching noises coming from his basket all night long. I turned on the TV to watch the news, idly wondering if in a few years' time, this might come courtesy of Malcolm Derby and his select group of investors. I checked my phone and found an email from Lina confirming that I would need to return to Florence for a couple of hours on Friday morning but, otherwise, I was okay to stay on here.

I found myself thinking yet again about Virginia, hoping that she would somehow come around to at least acknowledging my existence, even if she didn't decide she liked me. Anna meant a lot to me, and I knew that her daughter meant a lot to her. It would be great if we could become a happy family but, on the showing so far, I had a feeling that a rapprochement was as unlikely as Oscar giving up meat.

7

TUESDAY EARLY MORNING

I slept remarkably well, waking early to find Oscar stretched out
on the floor alongside the bed. For our morning walk, I took him
out of the main gate and turned left for a change. A farm track ran
parallel to the road almost as far as the edge of the trees that
marked the perimeter of the country park and Oscar and I chose
that, although at this time of day, there was little or no traffic on the
road itself. Partway along, I came upon an interesting scene. An old
gentleman was resting on the handle of a spade, staring intently at
a bright and shiny silver Fiat 500 parked just off the road. He was
wearing boots and faded blue overalls and, from the weather-
beaten look of his face, it was pretty clear he was a member of the
farming community. He barely took his eyes off the Fiat as I
approached but he did have the courtesy to reply to my greeting
before returning to studying the car, which was parked about
twenty feet off the road between two clumps of what looked like
bamboo cane. I've always had a curious streak so I stopped and
asked.

'New car?'

He shot me another quick glance before looking back at the car again. 'Looks like it, but what the hell's it doing here on my land?' He had lost quite a few teeth but he'd been left with two right in the middle of the top row and he reminded me vaguely of a chipmunk.

A thought occurred to me and I turned my head so I was looking back towards the villa. From here, I could see over the high perimeter wall and could just glimpse the top storey of the house and even the very top couple of feet of the pseudo Leaning Tower amid the trees. Suspicion began to grow in my head. A quick glance through the window showed me a Europcar sticker on the corner of the windscreen. Might this vehicle belong to somebody intent on spying on Malcolm Derby's meeting?

'Not your car, you say? Did you see who was driving it?'

He shook his head. 'If I had done, I would've said something to them. As it happens, I don't need to get my tractor in here today, but I might have done, mightn't I?'

'Do you live locally?'

He pointed to a farmhouse framed between two massive umbrella pine trees a couple of hundred metres away. 'That's my place there. What about you?'

'I live near Florence, but I'm staying at Villa Gregory for a few days. Are you going to be working near here this morning?'

By this time, he had transferred his attention from the car to me. 'Yes... why do you ask?'

'The owner of the property has hired me to check security. Would you mind doing me a favour?' I pulled out one of my visiting cards and handed it to him. 'If by any chance you see the owner of the car, could you take a good look at them and then give me a call?'

He studied the card for a few moments before looking up at me and giving me what my grandmother would have called a canny look. 'Private investigator, eh? What's going on in the villa, then? Something hush-hush?'

I had my story prepared. 'Nothing special, the owner just wants to be sure that the place is secure for when he does get people who need a bit of secrecy and privacy.'

This old boy clearly was no fool, but he didn't press me further and I saw him nod his head. 'If you say so. Anyway, I'm happy to help young Gus. His father was a miserable old so-and-so, but Gus is a good boy.' He reached into his pocket and pulled out a phone. 'I can do better than that. I'll take a photo of the guy and send it to you.'

I was mildly surprised that he carried a phone but, of course, these days nearly everybody does. Apart from me this morning. I suddenly realised I'd left mine beside the basin in the bathroom. I still had my notepad – as always – and I scribbled down the Fiat's registration number. The vehicle should be easy for the police to trace and, of course, in order to rent a car, the driver would have had to provide proof of identity. I thanked the old gentleman, who told me his name was Vincenzo Cascina, turned around, and headed back home, keen to collect my phone in case anybody had been trying to contact me.

As it turned out, they had.

I was walking along the drive past the side of the villa when the back door opened and Antonella appeared. She was in a terrible state.

'Dan! Thank God you've come back. We've been trying to call you. The most terrible thing's happened. There's been a murder.'

'There's been what?' It was a gormless question, but this had taken me completely by surprise. With all the security surrounding this meeting, the last thing I would have been expecting was this. Also, if true, it had happened on my watch and that gave me an uncomfortable feeling. 'Who's been murdered?'

'It's that young Englishman, the one who was wearing jeans last night.'

'Jonathan Farmer?' Virginia's boss, dead? I found myself secretly thankful that she, at least, hadn't been the victim. 'How did it happen?'

Antonella was looking quite overwhelmed. 'He's been stabbed... with a knife.'

'You're sure he's dead?'

I saw her take a couple of deep breaths. 'No question. I took him in his breakfast at eight and found him... It was awful. He's dead all right. Rocky's called the police and he's up there standing guard right now.'

'I'll go and take a look. Why don't you make yourself a cup of coffee and look after Oscar for me? You've had a serious shock. Sit down and take it easy.'

I followed her into the kitchen, left Oscar with her, and ran up the stairs to the first-floor landing. Corridors stretched away to the left and the right and I spotted a figure partway down the left-hand one. From his bulk, it was clear that this was Rocky. I hurried along to where he was standing by the door of one of the bedrooms. When he saw me, an expression of relief crossed his face.

'Dan, am I glad to see you! It's Signor Farmer. He's dead.'

Instinctively, I reverted to my previous incarnation. No longer was I a private investigator; I was once again a chief inspector in the murder squad. 'Who's been into the room?'

'Just Antonella and then me.'

'Was the door locked?'

'No. She knocked and then, when she got no answer, she turned the handle and the door opened. She looked inside, saw the man's body on the bed, and got a terrible shock.'

'I can imagine. And then she came running downstairs to call you?'

He nodded.

'Did she leave the bedroom door open?'

'No, she closed it behind her.'

'And locked it?'

He shook his head. 'To be honest, nobody bothers much with locking doors here at the villa. It's not like a hotel.'

'I understand. Have you or has she touched anything inside the room?'

'Absolutely not. Like I say, all either of us did was to peer in through the open door. We only touched the outside door handle.'

'Excellent...'

My attention was attracted by the sound of the door of the next room being opened and Virginia's head emerged. Seeing me, she deliberately switched her attention to Rocky and spoke to him in her impeccable Italian. 'What's going on? Has something happened? Is it Jon... Mr Farmer?'

Rocky glanced at me and I took over. Whether Virginia liked me or not, or wanted to speak to me or not, what had just happened was far more serious than a petty family feud.

'I'm afraid Mr Farmer's dead, Virginia.' I saw her eyes open wide in disbelief. 'He's been murdered.'

'What... how?' Her door opened fully and she took two steps towards us. She was wearing a pair of striped pyjamas and her feet were bare. The top button was missing and a piece of loose thread was hanging, but she was still decent.

I held out a cautionary hand. 'I'm sorry, but nobody's allowed into the victim's room. The police have been called and it's now a crime scene.'

'A crime scene? Are you sure he's been... murdered?' She sounded appalled. She stopped and just stood there looking shell-shocked. After a few moments, she glanced up at me. 'Who would do a thing like that?' In spite of the circumstances, I felt a little shot of relief that she felt able to speak to me directly so at least communication of some kind between us had finally been established.

I tried to sound reassuring. 'That's what the police will need to find out when they get here. Your room's right next door to his – did you hear anything last night? Did anything happen last night?' For a moment, I felt sure I saw a flicker of something cross her face – surely not guilt? A moment later, it had passed and I saw her shake her head.

'No, nothing happened.' Her face was expressionless. 'When you say murder, how was he killed?'

She was looking very vulnerable by now, so I chose my words carefully. 'I'm going in to take a look now. Why don't you go back into your room and get changed? I'm sure the police will want to question everybody when they get here.' I gave her an encouraging smile. 'Don't worry, they'll sort it out, I'm sure.'

For a fraction of a second, it looked almost as though she was thinking of giving me an answering smile, but then she just turned, went back into her room and closed the door. I glanced back at Rocky.

'I'm going to take a quick look around the victim's room. Would you stay here and make sure nobody else tries to come in?'

'Of course, you can count on me.'

He reached for the door handle but I stopped him. His wife had already touched it and his prints were probably already on it but, in case any traces remained of the murderer, I used a tissue to open the door and walked in. I turned and pushed it with the toe of my shoe until it was almost closed behind me. I didn't want to close it completely because I didn't want to touch the inside door handle when I left, but the murder scene had to be screened from the view of anybody in the corridor.

I stood there and took a long, slow look around. In fact, as murder scenes went, it wasn't too gruesome. The fully clothed body of Jonathan Farmer was splayed back across the bed with the handle of a knife protruding from his chest. The bed had not been slept in and he was fully clothed. There was some blood on his shirt and on a crumpled towel alongside the body, no doubt discarded by the killer, and, although there was a bit of staining on the bedcover, he had bled relatively little. From this, I deduced that the blade of the knife must have struck the heart, stopping it almost immediately. His facial expression was remarkably calm and he didn't appear to have put up a fight, which made me wonder if he'd been stabbed in his sleep. He was quite evidently dead but I went over and pressed a finger against his carotid artery anyway. There was no pulse, his skin was cold to the touch and his body was rigid. By my reckoning – but a pathologist would know better – he'd been dead for some time.

I straightened up and took a good look around. From the handle, it looked as though the murder weapon was a fairly intricate, possibly ancient dagger, and I remembered seeing the collection of these downstairs. Maybe the murderer had taken one of them. My attention was drawn to a band of lighter skin on the victim's left wrist. I checked the bedside table but it seemed pretty clear that his expensive watch had disappeared. Had he been robbed? If so, by the killer or somebody else?

The bedroom windows were closed, and the shutters and curtains were open but, interestingly, the light was still on. It looked as though the assault must have taken place while it was dark, possibly the previous night before Farmer had contemplated going to bed. From the amount he'd been drinking, it was possible that he hadn't bothered to undress or even close the blinds and had just crashed out on the bed, offering an unresisting target to his killer, who could easily have got in through the unlocked door.

Alternatively, maybe he'd returned to his room much later and had been attacked before he'd started undressing, possibly by a killer already hiding in his room, but that begged the question of where he'd spent the night. Had he been in somebody else's bed? For a moment, the suspicion crossed my mind that he might have been in Virginia's, but I did my best to stifle that thought until I had more proof. It was bad enough that she didn't want to talk to me because of my relationship with her mother, but if she thought I was considering her as a potential murderer, I felt sure that would only further damn me in her eyes.

The door to the luxurious en-suite bathroom was open and a quick glance inside revealed nothing untoward. As I turned back into the room again, I noticed that there was another door directly opposite the bathroom door. I didn't need the architect's plans of the house to realise that this had to be a communicating door between this bedroom and the one alongside.

And that belonged to Virginia.

I walked across and studied it closely without touching anything and immediately saw a rather fine ornate brass bolt that no doubt served to lock the door to protect the privacy of anybody in this room. The bolt was in fact open. Did this mean that Farmer had used it to go into Virginia's room or, awful as it was to imagine, could that have been the way that she had come in here to kill him? Once again, I made a conscious effort to discount this possible scenario. Virginia was Anna's daughter and I felt sure that she would never dream of committing murder... would she?

The sound of footsteps in the corridor attracted my attention and I straightened up and turned around. As I did so, the door was pushed open and I found myself confronted by a uniformed police officer with sergeant's stripes on her epaulettes and, just behind her, a large, red-faced man, who glared at me. He shouldered the sergeant out of the way and took two steps towards me, stabbing an accusing finger at me.

'What the hell are you doing in here? This is a crime scene. You shouldn't be in here. I could have you arrested, you know.' A big vein at his temple was throbbing and he looked as if he was about to explode. His jacket was hanging open and anybody familiar with the movies would immediately have recognised the curved handle of the huge revolver holstered below his left armpit. In fact, the weapon was so big, the barrel extended right down past his ample waist. It was a wonder he didn't shoot himself every time he sat down. With a sinking feeling, I realised that this had to be none other than Inspector Adolfo Vinci, described by Virgilio as a would-be tough guy and to be avoided like the plague. In an attempt to defuse the situation, I adopted an apologetic expression.

'I meant no harm. My name is Armstrong and I've been employed to look after security here at Villa Gregory.'

His eyes flicked towards the bloodstained body on the bed and a sneering tone entered his voice. 'Well, looks like you're pretty crap at your job, doesn't it? At least tell me you haven't touched anything.'

I did my best to stifle a rising feeling of antipathy towards this character and shook my head. 'Of course not, I know better than that. You see, I used to be—'

'Stop wasting my time and get out. Now!'

He gave me a dismissive gesture and, as I heeded his order, I caught a momentary flicker of what might have been sympathy on the face of his sergeant. Maybe she didn't approve of the inspector's bedside manner. I knew how she felt. I had spent two of my earlier years at Scotland Yard as a sergeant working for an Inspector Flynn, who had been one of the most unpleasant men I'd ever known; the sort of man who slapped suspects, swore at everybody, treated female officers as servants or worse, and who was finally thrown off the force for punching an innocent bystander. Inspector Vinci hadn't tried to punch me, but I wouldn't have put it past him.

Outside in the corridor, a little cluster of people had formed and another officer was standing with his back to the door, making sure that nobody came near. I spotted Gus Cornish amid the throng, looking far from cool, calm and collected this morning. Was this just natural shock or because of something he had seen or done, or was it just because a murder here at the villa would be very bad for business? I decided to herd them away and let the police get on with their job.

'If you'd all like to come down to the lounge, I'll tell you as much as I know.'

They turned, surprisingly obediently, and I was about to follow them when Virginia's door opened again. She was still looking dishevelled, but she had dressed in record time. As she came out, I glanced into her room and couldn't miss the sight of a chair wedged up against the handle of the door communicating with the victim's room. Did this indicate just a sensible precaution or had something happened? I remembered her hesitation when I had asked her that same question and I resolved to get her on her own and discover the truth.

Before the police did.

8

TUESDAY MORNING

Downstairs, I found a little group of people standing in the lounge. One was Antonella, still looking understandably shaken. I went across to her and adopted a comforting tone.

'Why don't you go and have a lie-down, Antonella? You've had a terrible shock and it'll help if you rest.'

She managed to muster a hint of a smile, but shook her head. 'Thank you, Dan, but I think I'd prefer to keep working. Why don't you and the others go through to the dining room? Breakfast's all laid out, and I'll go and make fresh coffee and tea.'

'Well, if you're sure. Do you want me to take Oscar off your hands?'

This time, a real smile appeared on her face. 'He's been ever so good. It's as if he knew I was upset. He's been sitting alongside me with his head on my knee. I think he would have climbed onto my lap if I'd let him. He really is a very good dog.'

'I'm glad to hear that. If you like, you're very welcome to hang onto him for now and when you get fed up with him, send him through to me. I'd better warn you, though, that if anybody wants bacon, you'll find him wherever that's being cooked. He has a thing for bacon rind – well, all food really, but bacon rind in particular.'

Her smile broadened. 'I was just going to do some bacon. Gus likes a traditional English breakfast and I expect some of the others will as well. I'll make sure Oscar gets at least the rind, if not more.'

This was clearly a woman who knew the way to my dog's heart. She went off to the kitchen and I herded the little group into the dining room. There were only four of them for now: Virginia, Piers, Eleanor Leonard and Eugenie, who was today dressed far more casually. All of them looked shaken by events and Piers was the first to speak up.

'So he really was murdered?' There was disbelief in his voice.

'I'm afraid so.' All eyes turned towards me. 'Mr Farmer was stabbed in the heart.' There were sharp intakes of breath around the room and I added a few words of consolation – insofar as words could help in a situation like this. 'He would have died almost instantly.'

As I spoke, I surveyed the four of them closely but could read little more than shock and horror, coupled with bewilderment, on their faces. This bewilderment was voiced by Eleanor Leonard. While she was speaking, I took a closer look at her. She was probably not that much older than Virginia, in spite of already having established a spectacular singing career. I remembered that she had been hailed as a child prodigy.

'But why? Who on earth would want to kill him, and how did they get in here?' Eleanor Leonard sounded as bamboozled as Piers.

A voice from the door answered her question and we all turned towards it. 'He was a very rich man and rich men have enemies.' It was Gus Cornish, still looking dazed – but not exactly saddened –

by the turn of events, but then I remembered his words the previous night. Clearly, he had had a low opinion of the victim. Low enough to commit murder?

'Any of his enemies here this week?' I couldn't help asking the question, although it generated another intake of breath around the room. I saw Cornish shake his head, but maybe not quite as decisively as I might have expected.

'Of course not, you surely can't suspect anybody here of doing anything so barbaric.' He walked across to where I was standing. 'We're all friends here.' He was doing his best to sound convincing but I, at least, felt sure I could detect a note of insincerity in his voice so I gave him a prod.

'So you're saying you think the killer must have got in from outside?' My thoughts went back to the silver Fiat out in the fields. Might that have belonged to the killer but, if so, how had he or she managed to get access over the wall and into the villa through presumably locked doors?

Cornish nodded decisively. 'It's the only explanation.'

I wasn't so sure, so I repeated the question to the others in the room. 'Can any of you think of anybody here this week who might have had a grudge against Mr Farmer?' They all shook their heads – although I felt I could sense a certain lack of sincerity in the room – so I tried another tack. 'What about what Mr Cornish just said? Can you think of anybody outside this group who might have had it in for Farmer? For now, let's leave out the question of how they could have managed to get into the villa to kill him.'

After a pregnant pause, Virginia was the first to speak up and I was gratified to see that she was actually managing to look me in the eye as she did so. 'Jon was a mercurial character, people either hated him or loved him, but I honestly can't think of anybody who could have hated him enough to stoop to murder.'

As his assistant, she almost certainly knew him better than anybody else here in the villa, so I tried to do a bit of digging. 'What about his private life? Was he married, divorced? Did he have girlfriends, boyfriends?'

Once again, I was sure I saw a shadow flit momentarily across her face. 'He wasn't married and, as far as I know, he wasn't in a serious relationship.' Her face and her tone darkened. 'He liked women, and there were a lot of them... a lot.'

If she hadn't been my girlfriend's daughter, I would have asked if she had been one of the many but I didn't, and any further questioning was interrupted by the arrival of a visibly perturbed Malcolm Derby and his wife.

'What's going on? There are police cars outside and police officers crawling all over the villa. What's happened?'

I told him. 'I'm afraid there's been a murder.'

He actually took a step backwards and I saw the blood drain out of his cheeks. If he was acting, he deserved an Oscar. Melanie at his side looked shocked but maybe to a lesser extent and when I gave them a brief summary of what had happened, both of them appeared dumbstruck. It was Piers who broke the silence.

'I was just going to text you with the news, Malcolm, but I didn't want to disturb you so early.' He was sounding most apologetic but all he got back from his boss was a dirty look.

'I would suggest that the small matter of murder is the sort of news that might be important enough for you to disturb me, don't you think, Piers?' His voice was heavy with irony, and I saw Piers cringe. Derby then turned his attention to me, and I braced myself for similar criticism but, to my surprise, he sounded almost complimentary. 'It seems I should have taken your advice and hired a squad of armed guards. Have you spoken to the police? Do they have any idea how the murderer managed to get in?'

I shook my head. 'They've only just arrived, but I find it hard to believe that somebody managed to make it over the wall and into the villa through locked doors without somebody noticing.'

He was an intelligent man and I didn't need to spell it out to him. As the ramifications of what I was suggesting struck home, his already pale complexion positively blanched.

'You think he might have been murdered by somebody here at the villa... by one of us?'

'I honestly don't know, but it's a consideration. Hopefully, the police investigation will get to the bottom of it.'

At that moment, the police arrived in the bulky shape of Inspector Adolfo Vinci, looking even redder in the face than before. He was accompanied by the same sergeant and I noticed that she kept her distance from him. Vinci stomped over to me and grabbed me roughly by the arm. 'You speak Italian. I want you to translate exactly every word I say. Got that?'

I reached over with my free hand and politely but firmly detached his grip on me. There's an effective way of doing this that I was taught at basic training. You squeeze the sides of the hand and it causes a sharp pain, making the aggressor release his hold. I managed to keep a friendly expression on my face, but it wasn't easy. 'I'm happy to act as interpreter, by all means. Fire away.'

Vinci neither thanked me nor acknowledged my offer, but I was gratified to see that he didn't try and grab me again. I was also pleased to see him massaging his hand. He cleared his throat noisily and was about to address the room when the door behind him opened and a flustered-looking Frau Baumgartner was ushered in by a police officer, closely followed by her husband. The only way it could have been more obvious that the financier was suffering from a serious hangover would have been if he had been carrying a placard. He looked like death warmed up. Seconds later, he was followed by Antoine Dujardin, who had abandoned his pink tuxedo this morning and was wearing trainers and a grey tracksuit, damp with sweat. Vinci waved to them to come over and join the rest of us before launching into his speech.

'As you may or may not know by now, there has been a murder.' As I translated, both Frau Baumgartner and Antoine Dujardin looked startled while Herr Baumgartner's face barely registered what they had just heard. I imagined he had enough on his plate with a throbbing headache to worry him, let alone a murder.

'The victim's name was...' Vinci consulted his notebook '... Jonathan Xavier Farmer. He was killed by a single stab wound to the heart. The murder weapon was one of a number of knives on display here at the villa and it has been taken away for forensic analysis.' Frau Baumgartner stared at him in disbelief while Dujardin looked appalled. 'The victim's room is now off limits to everybody.' He stared pointedly at me as he said these words before returning his attention to the rest of the group once more. 'Everybody currently staying or working at Villa Gregory is now confined to the premises. My officers will take your fingerprints and swab you for DNA, and you must surrender your passports until I authorise you to leave. My sergeant will come around to each of you to establish your movements last night. A serious crime has been committed, and there can be no exceptions. You will stay here in this room for now. Is that clear?'

To reinforce his point, he reached forward and banged his fist on the breakfast table. In so doing, he dislodged an egg from a little pyramid of eggs in a dish and we all looked on, mesmerised, as it rolled inexorably towards the edge of the table and dropped neatly onto the toe of his shoe. Unfortunately, at least in my opinion, it turned out to have been hard boiled, so it didn't break all over him. He rattled off a rapid series of colourful swear words –

Tuscans are good at swearing – and kicked the egg underneath the table. I assumed my helpful interpreter persona and caught his attention.

'Would you like me to translate what you've just said, Inspector?' I gave him my sweetest smile and his face darkened even more.

'Just do as you're told, goddammit.'

He had asked me to translate what he said, so I gave him an even sweeter smile and took him at his word, paraphrasing into English for the benefit of the others. 'The inspector is calling upon the Madonna, the saints and some assorted livestock to assist him in his investigation. He also doesn't like eggs.'

I caught the eye of the sergeant who was standing in the doorway and I thought I could detect a hint of a smile flash across her face. Clearly, her command of English was better than her superior's and she had a sense of humour – something that appeared to be singularly lacking in the inspector. He growled suspiciously at me and then picked up the narrative again, which I duly translated.

'While waiting for the services of an efficient professional interpreter...' he shot me an evil look '...I intend to do a thorough search of the whole building. This will include the bedrooms you have been occupying as well as your belongings.' A groundswell of protest began to build, but the inspector was having none of it.

'I give the orders here. Any one of you might be a murderer and I intend to find out who that was and see that they're punished to the full extent of the law.' I could see him eyeing the table again, but presumably his experience with the egg restrained him from banging his fist on it again.

A suave English voice broke the silence.

'Dan, I wonder if you'd be good enough to tell the inspector that it sounds to me as though he might be running the risk of exceeding his authority here.'

The sentence came from Gus Cornish and was delivered in measured terms. I knew that he spoke Italian better than I did and he could just as easily have said this to the inspector himself, but I could tell that Gus was playing to the crowd. Obediently, I translated for the benefit of the inspector and for a moment, I could have sworn I saw steam come out of the big man's ears. He was almost spluttering when he responded.

'I *am* the authority here. Tell the gentleman he would do well to remember that.' Inspector Vinci pointed an accusing finger at Gus and then stared belligerently around the room. 'I am the law around here.'

Still using restrained language and a neutral tone, Gus Cornish continued, undeterred, still directing his remarks to me to translate. 'And I'm the owner of this villa. I assume the inspector will have no objection to my calling Graziano Nobile, the Minister of Justice. I was dining with Graziano in Florence only a couple of weeks ago.'

Full marks to the inspector. Not only did his head not explode, but he also didn't climb down either. After a pause, presumably during which he was trying to get his blood pressure down from critical to just danger level, he fixed Gus Cornish with a malevolent stare and replied.

'In my opinion, a full search is absolutely necessary and I have instructed my officers to proceed immediately. You will all stay here. Nobody is to leave this room. I have no doubt that my superiors in the Ministry of Justice will back me up on this.'

If Oscar had been in the room, even he would have noted the uncertainty beneath the bluster in the big man's voice, but obviously Adolfo was one of those people who, when they get themselves into a hole, they just keep digging.

The inspector turned dismissively away and headed for the door. I waited until he and the sergeant had left before addressing my companions. 'At least until Mr Cornish can speak to the minister in Rome, I think we have to accept that we're being asked to stay in this room, so I suggest we have breakfast and let the police get on with their work.'

9

TUESDAY LUNCHTIME

It was a long morning, punctuated by a few rare bits of excitement. Just after nine, the sergeant came back with another officer and they took our fingerprints. I was professionally interested to see how they did it and, on a personal level, this was a first for me. I had taken hundreds of fingerprints over the course of my career and ordered many more thousands to be taken, but I had never been on the receiving end myself. When I first started out in the police force, fingerprints were taken by pressing the individual's fingers onto a black ink pad and then rolling each finger carefully onto a piece of card. It's still often done that way nowadays but I was interested to see that here in Pisa today, it was done digitally with a scanner and that way, none of us ended up having messy, black fingers. Even so, I could tell that most of my companions were very unhappy at being treated like potential murderers. Gus Cornish was still trying to get through to the Minister of Justice to put in a formal complaint but, either by chance or by design, the man was making himself difficult to pin down.

In comparison to her boss, the sergeant was polite and her English, while not fully fluent, was up to the task of getting everybody to describe their movements from dinner time last night until this morning. Unfortunately, I wasn't able to hear what was said by the others because these brief interviews were conducted in a corner of the room one by one. Wearing my 'former murder squad detective' hat, I would have loved to make a note of these for myself but, reluctantly, I had to accept that this investigation was out of my hands.

A rare bit of excitement was a moment of panic at ten o'clock when Piers and Malcolm Derby suddenly remembered that the big boss was supposed to be coming through on a video call, but all they had were their phones. I listened to Derby laboriously explaining to one of the richest and most powerful men in the world what had happened and that he and the rest of us were confined to one room until the local police managed to finish investigating the murder. I couldn't hear what Alexander Grunstock was saying, but it was pretty clear from the expression on Derby's face that his superior was extremely unhappy. Mind you, so were most of the people in the room.

Finally, around lunchtime, the search was completed. A number of other police vehicles had come and gone, including what was clearly a team of forensic investigators, and just before one o'clock the inspector came back with some astonishing news. He was positively purring with pride.

'You will all be relieved to know that I have identified and apprehended the murderer and he's being taken to the *questura* as I speak.'

I was genuinely amazed and unexpectedly impressed that the perpetrator was already in custody and on his way to the main police station. Maybe beneath Vinci's volcanic and theatrical exterior, there beat a real detective's heart. 'Congratulations, Inspector, that's excellent news. Do we know the murderer?'

The look he gave me was overflowing with self-satisfaction, but if he really had caught the killer so quickly, I suppose he could be forgiven at least some of his posturing. His tone when he replied was positively smug. 'Oh yes, you know him all right. His name is Riccardo Gentile.' He beamed at the other people in the room. 'As a matter of course, I'll be keeping your passports and would ask you to remain here at the villa until I've completed my enquiry, which shouldn't take long. Thank you for your cooperation.' His tone was dismissive and even the way he said thank you sounded fake.

It took me a few moments before I realised that when he spoke of Riccardo Gentile, he had to be talking about Rocky, who had told me his real name was Riccardo. A surname that translated as 'gentle' seemed singularly inappropriate for a man-mountain like that but it was the thought of him as the killer that genuinely surprised me. Rocky had worked here at the villa for years, so why on earth would he do something like this now? How did he know Jonathan Farmer, and what sort of grudge could he possibly have developed against the man? Apart from anything else, I rather liked Rocky and I found it hard to believe that he could be a cold-blooded killer. Still, for now, I had to accept the inspector's word, not least as it meant that we were all free to go about our business without being corralled in one room and bored to tears.

The inspector turned and almost tripped over Oscar, who had wandered over to greet the new arrival. The inspector gave an exasperated snort and for a moment, I thought he might even be about to aim a kick at my dog but, fortunately, he resisted the temptation. Oscar had emerged from the kitchen mid-morning with a wide, canine smile on his face, a bulging stomach, and a pervasive odour of bacon surrounding him. Unsurprisingly, the first thing he had done was to hunt down and devour the fallen, hard-boiled egg – shell and all – so as soon as the inspector had left, I hastened to take him out for a quick walk. I knew from experience that a

Labrador who has been eating boiled eggs can very quickly produce enough toxic gas to render an enclosed environment uninhabitable. After that, I wanted to go and see Antonella, who was no doubt in an awful state considering that her husband had just been arrested for murder.

Oscar and I went out into the parking area where the police vehicles were gradually moving off and I walked up to the main gate, turned right and right again so that we were in the fields once more. It was another lovely, sunny day, there wasn't a cloud in the sky, and the temperature was probably well into the high twenties by now. I made sure that we hugged the shade as much as possible – although there wasn't very much of it. Since getting Oscar almost two years earlier, I had soon learned one of the basic lessons of physics that dark colours absorb more heat than light ones. In consequence, in the middle of a hot, summer day, a black Labrador – even one born and bred here in Tuscany – can very quickly start to overheat.

We made our way along the narrow strip of bare earth between the field of corn and the brick wall surrounding the villa until we reached the little gateway I had spotted on Sunday and today, there was a surprise in store. The gate, which had previously been firmly bolted from the inside, was now hanging open, revealing the overgrown mass of greenery within. The faint path through the bushes that I had used the previous evening to check the bolts led off into the shrubbery towards the more open part of the grounds, but if somebody had used it more recently, they had left no clues behind. It must have been opened some time after my inspection, but whether for somebody to get out or to allow somebody to get into the gardens remained to be seen. Could there be a link between the open gate and the silver Fiat in the field? Rather than belonging to a nosey journalist, had it brought the killer? But if so, who and why? And how had the murderer managed to open the gate, which had been firmly bolted from the inside? Did this mean he or she might have an accomplice at the villa?

I took a couple of photos from the outside and again from the inside, carefully avoiding touching anything. It occurred to me that maybe the gate had already been investigated and left open by Forensics, who had come down here looking for clues, although I doubted if they would have spotted it behind the near impenetrable mass of greenery. Still, I knew there would be no harm in relaying the information to the police. Of course, since they claimed to have already got the murderer in custody, this might well turn out to be a red herring. Either way, from a security point of view, the sooner the gate was closed and bolted again, the better.

I headed back to the villa, hoping to catch one of the police officers before they all left, and I was relieved to find the same sergeant I had seen earlier, just about to get into the last remaining squad car. I went over to her and explained about the car in the field and the open gate. I dictated the registration number of the Fiat to her and she studied the photos I had taken. Finally, she looked up at me.

'Do you think any of this is significant?'

Oscar had positioned himself alongside her and she bent down to stroke his ears. He and I exchanged glances and I could see that we were both thinking the same thing – here was a much more approachable police officer than her boss.

'If the inspector hadn't already apprehended the person he believes to be the murderer, I think it might well have been important. How much proof do you have against Riccardo Gentile?'

I could see her eyes scrutinising me. She looked intelligent and I felt sure she was a good police officer. I had also got the impression earlier that she probably didn't find working for Inspector Vinci a bundle of laughs, and that further endeared her to me.

After a few moments, she nodded as if she had just made a decision and shot me a question.

'I understand from the owner of the property that you used to be a police officer in London. Is that correct?'

I nodded. 'Yes, I was in the Metropolitan Police murder squad.' I decided it wouldn't do any harm to mention my former rank. 'I was a detective chief inspector.' I used the English version of my title and I saw her nod in understanding.

'Chief inspector, that's the same as *commissario*, isn't it?' She gave me a little smile. 'So I should be calling you sir.'

'It's just Dan these days, Sergeant...' I checked her name badge '...Innocenti. That's interesting. I have a good friend in the police force in Florence called Innocenti – Marco Innocenti.'

Her smile broadened. 'Innocenti's quite a common name here in Tuscany, but I bet you mean my cousin, Marco. He's in the Florence murder squad and a sergeant as well. How do you know him?'

I gave her a brief account of a few occasions since moving to Italy almost two years earlier when I had helped Marco and, of course, his boss, Virgilio, and the smile stayed on the sergeant's face as she responded. 'I realise who you are now – my name's Paola, by the way. Marco told me about a case you had last year involving some crazy guy firing arrows at a bunch of Hollywood stars. That must have been fun.'

'Except for the poor guy that got shot, yes. Tell me, what evidence have you got against Rocky... Riccardo Gentile? I don't know the guy very well, but he really didn't strike me as the sort of person to commit murder. Maybe a punch or two, but not murder surely?'

I saw her eyes flick around, although it appeared that she was the last remaining police officer on the scene. 'To be honest, it's pretty shaky and circumstantial. The inspector reckons it's enough to charge him, but I'm not so sure.' She caught my eye for a moment. 'In fact, I'm sure it isn't, but the inspector does what the inspector does, and he doesn't need my advice.' She shrugged. 'Or at least, if I give it, he doesn't take it.'

Now why didn't that surprise me? I could well imagine that misogyny would form part of Vinci's arsenal. 'Just what have you got against Gentile?'

'A Rolex watch belonging to the victim was found in the pocket of a jacket belonging to Gentile. Also, he has a record.'

'A criminal record? For what?'

'He was involved in a brawl in a beachside café in Viareggio five years ago. He punched some guy, broke his nose and fractured his eye socket. He pleaded self-defence, got probation and he didn't go to jail.'

'I see. And were his prints on the watch?'

'Forensics say it was wiped clean.'

'And where was the jacket?'

'That's the thing, it was hanging in the hall. Like I told the inspector, anybody could have put the watch in there. There's no way the public prosecutor will allow a case like this to go to court.' She took another cautious look around. 'In fact, I have a feeling it won't even go as far as the public prosecutor. Just as the inspector was leaving ten minutes ago, he got a call from the station. He didn't say who it was, but he didn't look happy.'

I wondered if this meant that Gus Cornish had finally managed to speak to his friend, the Minister of Justice. If so, I could only imagine the sort of pressure that Inspector Vinci was going to find himself under now. In spite of his irascible, high-handed manner, I almost felt sorry for him. I could still remember two cases in particular during my time at Scotland Yard when I'd been leant on in a big way by some very powerful politicians. Me being me, I had ignored them – to my cost. One of my failings from a career point of view had always been a reluctance to kowtow to people in positions of importance. The fact that I had never made superintendent was at least partly due to an innate unwillingness to brown-nose the right people. Still, at least it had meant I could sleep at night. I glanced at Innocenti.

'I was impressed by your English. You managed the interviews well and I could see you understood what I was saying when I was talking to the others.'

She shrugged her shoulders. 'I get by with the simple stuff, but it's only what I learned at school and a few evening classes really.'

'Well, if the case against Gentile fails and you need help interviewing anybody here at the villa in more depth, I'll be happy to help out.' I pulled out one of my cards and gave it to her. 'My mobile number's on there. Just call if you need anything.'

She gave me another smile and a smart salute before opening the car door. 'Thank you, *Commissario*. Now I need to get back to the station.' She caught my eye. 'I have a feeling you and I'll be meeting again very soon.'

I hurried back into the villa to look for Antonella. I found her slumped over the kitchen table and Oscar immediately made a beeline for her side, sat down and placed one big, black paw on her lap. She caught hold of it and looked up at me.

'*Ciao*, Dan. You've heard the news?' Her face was blotchy and there were fresh tears on her cheeks.

I pulled up a chair and sat down alongside her. 'Yes, but it's nonsense. I've just been speaking to one of the police officers who tells me the evidence is circumstantial at best. You wait and see: Rocky will be back home by tonight.'

An expression of hope appeared on her face. 'Do you really think so? It can't have been Rocky. He'd never do anything of the sort. People take one look at him and they think he's some kind of monster but he's a sweetie. I know he wouldn't have done it and I'm not just saying that because I'm married to him.'

'Well, if it helps, I can tell you that I don't think he did it either. Can you think of anybody who might have done it, though? The police haven't given a time of death yet but by my reckoning it was almost certainly last night as people were going to bed.' I threw out a battery of questions. 'What time did you go to bed? Did you see anything suspicious or anybody wandering around who shouldn't have been? Mr Cornish is convinced that it has to be somebody from outside – do you think anybody could have got in without being noticed?'

She shook her head decisively. 'No chance at all. Rocky and I were both up until midnight. He went out in the car at eleven to take the chef to his hotel in town, but he was back by twenty past. A few of the guests went down to the pool for a swim so we waited until they came back inside before we did the rounds, locking doors and windows. There's no way anybody could have got in after that.'

Unless somebody inside the villa let them in. If so, who? I carried on questioning Antonella. 'Do you have any thoughts about who might have done it? Did you notice any of the guests behaving strangely last night?'

I saw her stop and reflect for a few moments. 'Not really. The man who got killed was very drunk but then, so was the older Swiss gentleman. When I was clearing up at the end of the meal, I needed a bucket and a mop to clear where the Swiss man had been sitting. The terrace around him was covered in fallen bits of food and was awash with spilt wine.' She managed to produce a little smile. 'I expected a Swiss to be tidier than that, but it hardly makes him a murderer. I thought the Canadian woman was a bit strange, but that was probably her clothes as much as anything else.'

'Nobody looking suspicious, worried, preoccupied?'

'The very pretty girl with the long, dark hair – I think she was the victim's assistant – I thought she was looking preoccupied.'

I nodded in agreement but didn't go into detail about how in fact *I* had almost certainly been at least part of the root of Virginia's preoccupation. 'Anybody else?' She shook her head and I returned to what she had said earlier. 'Why doesn't the chef stay here at the villa like I do?' This sounded suspicious, but her explanation appeared to clear the Frenchman.

'Emile brought his wife with him and she wanted to see the sights of Pisa, so Gus put them up in a hotel in the *centro storico*.'

'And where is Emile today? Shouldn't he be here preparing lunch?'

'Under normal circumstances, yes, but we called him and told him to stay away until the police give us the go-ahead. Have the police cleared off completely now? I must ring him. As Rocky isn't here, he'll have to take a taxi.'

That would appear to clear the chef of any suspicion although, of course, he might have made his way back again after being dropped off at his hotel by Rocky. Maybe he had opened the gate in advance and then slipped back in to kill Farmer. However, this seemed highly unlikely, not least because I was unaware of any motive he might have had. Thinking aloud, I shot a few more questions at Antonella.

'What about earlier in the evening? Could anybody have got in before then? While we were all outside on the terrace having our meal, were the doors locked or unlocked?'

Again, she shook her head. 'The front door and the back door lock automatically when they close and can only be opened from the inside by using the handle, or from the outside with a key. No, I really can't see how somebody could have got in.'

I decided it wouldn't hurt to mention the open back gate and she looked surprised. 'That shouldn't have been like that, but it's so overgrown down there, I suppose Rocky rarely checks it. Gus is always very insistent that the gates should be kept locked at all times.' She looked up from Oscar, who had subsided onto the floor at her feet. 'It's bolted on the inside so that it can't be opened from the outside, so are you saying somebody here opened it? It certainly wasn't me and I'm sure it wasn't Rocky.'

'Well, it wasn't me either so that means we're left with...' I did a quick bit of mental arithmetic '...ten possible suspects. Take your pick.'

10

TUESDAY AFTERNOON

When I got back to the apartment, I phoned Anna to tell her what had happened. In fact, she already knew because Virginia had called her a little while before and Anna was sounding understandably concerned.

'I just wish I could come there right now but I have classes all afternoon and I'm booked to give a talk to the University of the Third Age this evening. Hopefully, I'll be able to get away tomorrow after lunch. Virginia said the police have arrested the murderer. Do you think that'll be the end of it?'

I hesitated, but then decided it was only fair to tell her what I thought. 'I'm afraid the police inspector handling the case thinks he's God's gift to policing but I've a feeling he isn't too bright. It looks very much to me as though he's arrested the wrong man.'

'Are you saying that you think the murderer might still be in the villa?' I could hear the fear in her voice and I could understand it. Her only daughter's boss had just been murdered, so might Virginia be next in line? From what she said next, Anna wasn't only worried for her daughter. 'It's a frightening thought. What if it happens again, and next time it's Virginia or *you*?'

I hastily did my best to reassure her. 'It's not definite that it was somebody from the villa.' I told her briefly about the car in the field and the open gate. 'But, even if it is somebody here, it's quite clear that the murder victim wasn't universally popular. As one of the guys here said, he was very rich, and rich people have enemies. I think we can safely assume that Farmer was the target and, now that he's been killed, the murderer will only be intent on trying to remain undetected.'

'Oh God, I do hope you're right.'

A few moments after the call ended, I got a text message from an unknown number. It turned out to be an unexpectedly formal-sounding message from the old gentleman I had met this morning by the little Fiat.

Dear sir. I'm sorry to inform you that while my attention was taken trying to mend one of the irrigation sprinklers, the owner of that car managed to drive off in it. All I saw was a distant figure of a man, definitely a man. Apologies I can't be more helpful and good hunting. Vincenzo Cascina

I gave a frustrated snort before sending him back a message with my thanks. Hopefully Europcar would be able to provide details of the driver of the rental car. The trouble was that I still couldn't see how this person – assuming that he had been a hired killer – had been able to get through the gate that could only be opened from inside and make his way unseen into the villa. Every-thing pointed to an accomplice inside and, as I had told Antonella, that gave us ten people to choose from.

I gave Oscar his lunch and then handed him the bone from last night. His eyes opened wide in wonder as he took it reverently from my hand and settled down by the empty fireplace to enjoy it. To an accompaniment of frightening cracking noises – I was getting used to this by now, but when I first gave him a bone, I had been very worried that he might break his teeth but they were clearly made of sterner stuff – I made myself a ham and cheese sandwich and sat down to reflect on the events of the morning.

I wondered how many people would mourn the passing of Jonathan Farmer. From what Virginia had said, there probably wasn't a wife or loved one shedding tears over his death and, from the frosty reaction of most of the other guests here when he had appeared last night, I had a feeling there were probably quite a few people in the business community who would actively welcome his removal from the financial scene. The big unknown was whether there was anybody here in the villa who had felt strongly enough about him to kill him or to hire a killer to do their dirty work for them. It is, after all, a massive step from dislike, envy or resentment to planning and carrying out a murder.

I let my mind run over the people I had met here. I was increasingly convinced that neither Rocky nor his wife fell into the murderer category. For my own personal reasons – not that they would have stood up in a court of law – I also dismissed Virginia... well, almost. I knew I wanted to have a long talk to her about her relations with her boss and, in particular, just exactly what might or might not have happened last night via the communicating door.

I was also tempted to exclude Malcolm Derby and his wife from the list of serious suspects. In his case, I couldn't see what possible advantage he could have hoped to gain by killing the man who had almost certainly been the wealthiest of all his potential investors. As far as Melanie was concerned, I just couldn't see her as a killer, although I knew to my cost that appearances can be deceptive. As for the others, it was less clear.

I felt pretty sure that there had been considerable surprise among the other reactions I had noted on the faces of the others when Farmer had appeared on the terrace the previous night. Along with surprise had been definite antipathy and I wondered whether Malcolm Derby, either accidentally or on purpose, had omitted to circulate a complete list of attendees in advance of the meeting. In view of Farmer's less than stellar reputation in the business community, Derby had no doubt been afraid that some or even all of the others might have refused to participate if they had known with whom they would be having to fraternise.

Of the others, Dujardin had been the most openly hostile while the Swiss lady and the opera singer had studiously avoided looking at him. Mind you, Melanie Derby and Eugenie hadn't looked too enamoured of him but that might just have been because of his shameless flirting at the table. It would be interesting to know exactly why so many people had seemed to dislike the man and I pulled out my phone and rang Paul.

Paul Wilson, my good friend and my former sergeant at Scotland Yard, was now an inspector and on occasions I had sought his help in getting background information about suspects in other cases. He had always been most obliging, although I tried not to bother him unless it was important. Considering that I was increasingly convinced that an innocent man was currently languishing behind bars, I felt it my duty to involve myself with the investigation – although I had little doubt that Adolfo Vinci wouldn't see it that way.

Paul sounded pleased to hear from me and we chatted for a few moments before I told him there had been a murder. I gave him the names of the people here at the meeting and asked if he could give them a quick health check. 'In particular, I'd really like to know if there's any reason why any of them might have had it in for the victim. I definitely got the impression Jonathan Farmer, the victim, wasn't flavour of the month with all of them.'

The name rang a bell with him immediately. 'Is that Jonathan Farmer, the guy the tabloids call the "Playboy Billionaire"?'

'The very same.'

'Wow, this is big! Leave it with me, Dan, I'll see what we can dig out. Certainly when this news hits the media, there's going to be all hell let loose, not just here but globally. He was a big name.'

'At the moment, I don't think the news has been released. Certainly if I were the investigating officer, I'd be trying to keep it all under wraps for now to avoid a mass of journalists and paparazzi descending on the villa.' I hesitated for a moment. 'Although the inspector here who's dealing with the case doesn't strike me as being the sharpest tool in the box, so who knows what he'll do?'

What the inspector did next came as a considerable – and unwelcome – surprise to me.

A few minutes after three o'clock in the afternoon, I was sitting in the kitchen with Antonella while Oscar leant lovingly against her legs as she stroked his head. I'd had my work cut out dragging him away from the bone, which in the space of a couple of hours had been almost halved in size, but he had reluctantly agreed to be separated from it – temporarily. There was the sound of a bell and she got up and went across to a panel on the wall and pressed the intercom button.

'Yes, who is it?'

A male voice answered. 'Police. Let us in.'

She pressed the gate-release button and turned back towards me. 'Now what do they want?'

I tried to sound optimistic. 'Maybe they've brought your husband back.'

And that was exactly what they had done, but it turned out not to be the only reason they had come. I walked out with her to the front door and we saw two squad cars pull up outside. The doors opened and Rocky, now no longer in handcuffs, jumped out and hurried across to hug his wife warmly while she sobbed into his chest. I waited until he stepped back from her before asking the obvious question.

'Does this mean they've dropped charges against you?'

He looked across at me and nodded. 'Grudgingly, yes. Mind you, it's just as well I wasn't hoping for an apology from that fat bastard.' He shot Inspector Vinci a look that was positively caustic, but the inspector didn't see it. He had other things on his mind.

Adolfo stomped across towards me with a couple of uniformed officers at his heels and jabbed me in the chest with his finger. 'Daniel William Armstrong, I'm arresting you for the murder of Jonathan Xavier Farmer.' He turned to one of the officers beside him. 'Handcuff him.'

I thought I had seen most things in my time but I have to confess that this had me completely flabbergasted. 'You're doing what?'

Adolfo was looking positively smug. 'I'm arresting you. You thought you were so clever, but nobody outsmarts me.' He waved to his officers. 'Take him away, men.'

My hands were pulled behind my back and I felt the cuffs being attached. I did a bit of quick thinking, which wasn't easy because I was still feeling totally gobsmacked. I knew the guy was an idiot, but two miscarriages of justice in one day was pushing it. I exchanged glances with Rocky and saw him roll his eyes. 'Can you look after Oscar for now? And please will you ring my office and speak to Lina, my PA? She'll know what to do.'

And the first thing I hoped she would do would be to contact her husband in the Florence murder squad in the hope that he could sort out the mess his Pisan counterpart was making of this investigation.

11

TUESDAY AFTERNOON

The *questura*, or central police station, in Pisa is a square block, painted in a mixture of ochre colours, situated just outside the historic centre of the city and topped by a mast bristling with antennae. To get there, we drove past the impressive medieval stone walls of the old city within which lay the Leaning Tower but, today, I was in no mood for sightseeing. The squad car turned in through the tall gates into the car park and I was ushered inside. The custody sergeant relieved me of my personal possessions, meticulously listing them by hand and then making me sign for them. This at least had the advantage that the handcuffs had to be removed and I was able to massage my wrists. Sitting in a car with your arms behind your back puts quite a lot of strain on the wrists and although I had tried handcuffs back in basic training, being driven around while wearing them was a new experience. And one I would be more than happy not to repeat any time soon.

I was led through a steel door and along a narrow corridor. It was hot and clammy and there was that same lingering mixture of disinfectant and sweat in the air that took me right back to prison visits I had made in my time. Only, on those occasions, I had been visiting the prisoners and this time I was one of them. Halfway down the corridor, the officer in front of me stopped and opened a grey, steel door with a key attached by a chain to his waist.

'Welcome to Hotel Pisa.' He gave me a grim smile. 'Hope you enjoy your stay in our beautiful city.'

I stepped inside and heard the door clang shut behind me. I found myself in a six-foot-by-eight-foot box with a narrow bed along one wall, a stainless-steel toilet without a seat at the far end and nothing else. The walls were concrete blocks painted a dismal shade of beige and there was a letter-box-shaped window about three feet by less than a foot situated well above eye level. I could see a grill on the outside of this, presumably to prevent people with a much slimmer physique than mine from somehow scrambling up and out. I looked back at the door and saw a peephole and a slot through which I assumed I would be served my next meal – if I was lucky.

I sat down on the hard bunk and took stock. They say that new experiences are what makes life interesting but at this particular moment, I knew I would have been happy to have done without the novelty. It was a sobering experience in many ways. For the first time, I found myself in the same position as so many suspects with whom I'd had dealings over the years. Some of these had been guilty, some not guilty, some truly deserving of punishment and others who had either fallen under the malevolent influence of evil people or poor fools whose mental faculties hadn't been up to the stresses and strains of life. I glanced at my watch instinctively but all I saw was my empty wrist. The watch, along with my phone and wallet, was now in a safe custody box at the other end of the corridor. I did a bit of calculation, working out that it had been just after three when I had gone to see Antonella, so presumably it had to be somewhere between three-thirty and four now.

I leant back against the refreshingly cool wall and hoped that

Rocky or his boss would by now have been able to relay details of my predicament to Lina. I had little doubt that the first thing she would do would be to contact her husband, but then the question was what he could do. Although Virgilio was a senior police officer in Florence, Pisa was out of his jurisdiction and, just as I used to hate having officers from other forces meddling with my cases, I could imagine considerable resistance from our friend Adolfo Vinci if Virgilio were to try to horn in on his case. The next problem was to work out exactly what his case was. Why had he arrested me? Surely it had to be more than plain animosity. Even a nincompoop like Vinci would surely need proof of some sort.

I tried to think myself into the investigating officer's head. From what Sergeant Innocenti had told me at lunchtime, he had probably been leant on by his superiors to get a quick result and no doubt had been instructed to avoid ruffling the feathers of a group of very important people. In consequence, trying to pin it onto first Rocky and now a random private investigator had seemed like sensible choices to him. His problem was surely going to be proof, or the lack of it. I sat there and tried to think what I might have done that could have given him the idea that I was Farmer's killer. Yes, he had found me in the room on my own standing by the victim that morning, but the body was clearly suffering from rigor mortis and had been dead for many hours. I would surely have been an immensely stupid murderer to stand there all night long waiting for the inspector to appear.

Of course, my fingerprints had been on the bolts on the little gate and were all over the villa from when I had done my bug sweeps, but I felt sure that there was no way the public prosecutor would see that as proof of guilt, not least as most of the time, I had been accompanied by Rocky. A sudden memory came back to me: the weapons in the music room. I had definitely handled three or four of the knives and daggers from the rack on the wall but, fortunately for me, if one of them turned out to be the murder weapon, Rocky had been with me and, again, he could attest to my innocence. Maybe this was it, although surely any murderer with half a brain would either have worn gloves or would have wiped their prints off the dagger before leaving the scene, and doing this would obviously have removed my prints at the same time. Otherwise, I couldn't think of any other reason Vinci might have to believe me to be the killer. However, I had come across enough occasions of miscarriages of justice in my time to be more than a little bit concerned all the same. Still, I told myself that worrying about it wouldn't do me any good, so I closed my eyes and tried to think about other things.

I thought about my little house in the hills, my daughter, long walks with Oscar and, of course, I thought about Anna. Thinking about her made me think of her daughter and I couldn't shake the suspicion that Virginia knew more than she was letting on about the murder. I was still resolutely avoiding going so far as to entertain the thought that she might have stabbed her boss, but I felt convinced that she had more to tell. As for the identity of the murderer, I was no further forward but, deep down, I was convinced that either Dujardin, the Baumgartners, Augustus Cornish or even the beautiful Eleanor Leonard held the key. I sincerely hoped that Paul back at Scotland Yard would be able to dig up some dirt about one of them.

I probably sat there for the best part of an hour before I had a visitor. To my surprise, this was neither the inspector nor a custody officer sent to escort me to an interview room. It was Sergeant Innocenti and she was carrying a cup of coffee in one hand and a croissant in the other. She came in and gave me a wry smile.

'Here, I thought you might like a snack.' The door behind her was still open and I glimpsed the face of a uniformed officer standing outside. She was no doubt aware of this; I could tell she was measuring her words. 'Sorry to see you in here. The inspector will be interviewing you pretty soon and hopefully, we'll be able to get to the truth.'

I took the coffee and the croissant from her and gave her a smile. 'I'm sure it'll all be sorted out soon. At least this gives me a new experience to use in one of my murder-mystery books.'

She looked surprised. 'You're a writer?'

'Just starting out. It's sort of a new career for me.' I let my eyes flit over her shoulder to the officer in the corridor behind her. 'Thanks for the coffee, but you probably shouldn't be in here, should you?'

She smiled back and turned towards the door, stopping as she reached it. 'It'll all work out, I'm sure.'

The door closed behind her, and I heard the key turn in the lock. Reflecting that it was comforting to know that I would appear to have at least one ally in here, I sipped the *caffé latte* – which tasted a damn sight better than the coffee in my old nick – and nibbled the croissant. I was just nearing the end of it when I noticed something written on the flimsy paper serviette in which it had been wrapped. I looked at this more carefully and saw that it appeared to be a handwritten message. Conscious of the peephole in the door, I stood up and turned so I was facing away from it while I separated the serviette from the croissant and flattened the paper in my palm to read it. It was brief but encouraging.

He has nothing against you that will stick. He's just desperate.
I've texted my cousin Marco. You'll be out soon. Courage!

The word *coraggio* doesn't just mean courage in Italian. It means *don't worry, things are going to be all right*. It's the sort of thing you say to a child about to take an exam or to somebody going to the dentist. It was definitely encouraging to know that she had notified her cousin so, one way or another, the Florence murder squad were definitely aware of what was going on. What they would be able to do about it was another matter.

It was very kind, but also risky, of Paola Innocenti to pass me this message and the last thing I wanted was for her to get into trouble so I carefully tore the piece of paper where the message was written away from the rest of the serviette, wrapped it around the last piece of croissant and popped it into my mouth. It was a bit chewy but it didn't taste unpleasant and, with the aid of another mouthful of coffee, I managed to swallow the evidence. As it went down my throat, I reflected that it would have been useful to have had my Labrador here. When it comes to swallowing evidence – and anything else, for that matter – he's unbeatable. Thought of Oscar made me realise how much a part of my life he'd now become, and I missed having his company. Hopefully, I would be reunited with him before long.

For now, all I could do was wait.

12

TUESDAY EARLY EVENING

The time on the clock on the interview room wall was showing six-thirty exactly when Inspector Vinci came in and sat down heavily on the chair opposite me. The uniformed officer who had brought me from my cell was now standing behind me, impassive. There was an apparatus with a familiar battery of buttons on the table so that the session could be recorded and a mirror on the wall behind the inspector through which I knew I was probably being filmed. To my surprise, however, he made no attempt to start any recording. Instead, he just subjected me to a malevolent stare.

'Signor Armstrong, you have some powerful friends.'

This sounded promising. 'That's good to hear, Inspector. And what did my powerful friends tell you?'

'They told me that you didn't kill Signor Farmer.'

Definitely promising. 'Well, they're right. I most certainly didn't kill him, just in case you still have any doubts. The fact that my prints were all over the place was because I was employed to do a security sweep of the villa, working my way through all the rooms. I may even have touched the murder weapon on the music-room wall, but I was with a witness when I inspected the rack of daggers.'

He nodded a few times. 'I see. Apparently, you work with the Florence murder squad. They've vouched for you.' His tone was grudging – at best.

'I've worked alongside them a few times, but that still doesn't prove I'm innocent. I'm sure we've both come across enough rogue police in our time. For all I know, you yourself might have a few bodies in the freezer back home.' His face darkened but I carried on. 'Anyway, like I say, I didn't do it and, although for some reason you don't appear to like me, I'm on your side and I want to solve this murder just as much as you do. I'm willing to help in any way I can.'

His expression softened – a fraction. 'Thank you, but that will not be necessary. I prefer to work alone.'

'Are you following any leads?'

He shook his head importantly. 'That's no business of yours. I'm in charge of this investigation and I expect you to remember that.'

I nodded. 'Understood, Inspector. Can I just ask if your people have checked the details of a rental car that I saw parked in the fields beyond the villa?'

I saw him consider the request before grudgingly opening the folder he had brought with him. 'The Fiat 500 was rented yesterday at seventeen hundred hours by a Lawrence Richard Butler, domiciled in Chicago, USA. He's currently staying at the Hotel Imperial here in Pisa and I'm just about to go and visit him.'

'Do you need an interpreter? I'm happy to help out if needed.'

He shook his head. 'No, we have our own interpreters. You can go.' He stood up and indicated the door with his finger. 'That's the way out.'

I stood up as well. 'Can I take it that I'm no longer under suspicion?'

He took his time before answering. 'That is correct. Good day, Signor Armstrong.' Just like Rocky, I wasn't going to get an apology either, but that didn't come as a surprise.

The first thing I did after getting my belongings back was to go outside onto the pavement and call Virgilio in Florence.

'*Ciao*, Virgilio, I'm out. I imagine I have you to thank for that.'

I heard him chuckle. 'You not only have me to thank, but you also have to thank Marco Innocenti and the *Questore*.'

'Wow, you certainly got the big guns out. The *Questore* no less. How did you swing that?' The *Questore* was the equivalent of the Commissioner or Chief Constable over in Britain. A big gun indeed.

'He has a long memory. He knows that we owe you for all those times you've helped us out. Also, off the record, your friendly local inspector there in Pisa has made a bit of a reputation for himself for being an idiot. Apparently, he's just one more cock-up away from being sent to the wilds of Calabria or the Badlands of Sicily. Anyway, my *Questore* called his *Questore* and I'm delighted to see that the result is that you're a free man. What are the Pisa cells like? Probably as unappealing as the ones we have here.'

Now that I was out, I could afford to be magnanimous. 'Everything was okay and everybody was fine. Even the inspector mellowed a tiny bit by the end. When I say "mellowed", I mean maybe just dialled it back a bit from Genghis Khan to, say, Ivan the Terrible. Anyway, thank you very much indeed for getting involved, and big thanks to Marco as well. His cousin's a sergeant here and she's been a great help. And, of course, do say thank you to the big boss. Sorry to give you extra work.'

'I gather some big-noise financier has been murdered there. If you didn't do it – and I'm going to look pretty silly if you did – who might have? Got your eye on anybody?'

I gave him a quick rundown of the runners and riders and told him I had contacted Paul in London. 'I'm hoping he can find some kind of a motive for somebody in the house to have been our killer. There's just a possibility it was done by somebody from outside, and Inspector Vinci is interviewing a man as we speak, but my money's still on it being an inside job. Fingers crossed that Paul manages to dig something up.'

The next call was to Anna, but it went to voicemail and I felt it best not to leave a message telling her I had just emerged from police custody so I just rang off and vowed to try again a bit later.

I had only just come off the phone when a smart, red Alfa pulled up alongside me and the window opened. I looked inside and saw that it was Sergeant Paola Innocenti.

'I heard that the inspector had released you.' She gave me a knowing look. 'From what I could gather, you have friends in high places.'

I reached into the car and shook her hand warmly with both of mine. 'Not just in high places. I need to say a big thank you to you for your note. It's the first time I've been locked in a cell and it was good to know that I had somebody on my side.'

'You're very welcome. I passed on the information about the rental car to one of my people and I believe the inspector is interviewing the guy now. Let's hope that gives us a lead, because Forensics have come up with very little. Your prints were on the handle of the dagger but the murderer clearly wore gloves as they were slightly smudged. They're doing a full post-mortem and a detailed check of the body this evening just in case something unexpected crops up but, if that doesn't bring any results, we're a bit stuck.'

'Did the pathologist establish time of death?'

She nodded. 'He said a three-hour window roughly between 10 p.m. and 1 a.m.'

This meant I'd probably been right in my supposition that Farmer had almost certainly been killed on his way to bed after a cocktail of alcohol and drugs. 'From the way he was lying on the bed and the expression on his face, I got the feeling he was probably asleep when he was assaulted. He'd been drinking heavily and for my money, he had been snorting cocaine. Did the pathologist say anything about that?'

She nodded again. 'He said exactly the same thing. Even without doing the autopsy, he said the whole body reeked of alcohol and there were traces of cocaine in the man's nostrils. He said the guy was probably so stoned that he just crashed out on the bed. There were no signs of resistance and no lacerations to his hands from where he might have tried to deflect the blade, so all the murderer had to do was stick the knife in.'

'Which means that anybody could have done it, not necessarily a big, strong man.'

'Indeed, but it must have been someone with a strong stomach; stabbing somebody in cold blood isn't for the faint-hearted. The problem is that this doesn't help us whittle down the suspects, does it?' She glanced at her watch. 'I'm just going off duty now. Would you like a lift somewhere? Back to the villa?'

'Only if it's not taking you out of your way. I can take a taxi.'

'Not at all. I'm picking my son up from his grandma and she lives out that way.'

I climbed in and she drove me back through the evening traffic towards the villa. We chatted and I discovered that she had a husband, who was a doctor at the local hospital, and a four-year-old son. I told her a bit about my past troubles where my job back in London had effectively scuppered my marriage, but she sounded remarkably upbeat about her chances.

'Gianni and I both have pretty full-on jobs but we make it work. Having two sets of grandparents in the town to provide childcare is a major bonus.'

She was easy to talk to and I soon found myself telling her more about my writing and how I'd fallen in love with Tuscany and had decided to settle over here. She, on the other hand, told me how much she loved England and how her dream was to go and live over there one day. We human beings are a funny bunch.

She dropped me outside the villa and, after I'd thanked her again and she had driven off to collect her son, I let myself in through the main gate and walked around to the side of the villa. When I reached the kitchen door and tapped on it, I heard Oscar's familiar part-howl-part-yawn-part-woof that indicated that he had realised who was on the other side of the door. This was opened by a tall man, made even taller by the fact that he was wearing a white chef's hat on his head.

Oscar, tail wagging furiously, stood up on his hind legs and pawed at my belt, clearly as pleased to see me again as I was to see him, although I felt sure that if he had had to choose where to be abandoned, a kitchen would probably have been about as good as it got. The chef looked pleased to see me.

'You must be Chief Inspector Armstrong. I'm glad you've come back.' His English was very fluent, although his accent instantly labelled him as French.

'It's just Dan these days. And you must be Emile. I wanted to come and see you last night to compliment you on a stunning meal, but I got waylaid. Thank you very much.'

He gave me a self-deprecating smile, but the compliment had clearly hit home as his smile broadened. 'I'm very pleased you enjoyed the meal and I imagine that Oscar here enjoyed the remains of the lamb.' Hearing his name, Oscar wandered over to the chef and rubbed his head against his knee.

'The way to a Labrador's heart is through his stomach.'

'Anyway, Dan, I'm delighted you're back because now I hope you can take your lovely dog out of my kitchen. Please.'

'Of course, Health and Safety definitely wouldn't approve.'

He gave a very Gallic shrug. 'That's not it. It's just that I don't like people observing me closely when I'm cooking, and ever since I started preparing this evening's meal, I've had a constant shadow by my feet. I swear I can feel his eyes boring into the back of my head whenever I handle food.'

I had to laugh at that. He had got Oscar bang to rights. I thanked him for putting up with my four-legged friend and took Oscar out for a walk around the grounds. Out of curiosity, I headed back to the little gateway in the end wall, pushing through the dense undergrowth until I could see that it had been firmly bolted once more. What's that old expression about shutting the stable door? The path through the bushes was a bit wider now and to my trained eye, it looked to me as though Forensics had been here. I wondered if they'd been able to get any prints off the gate – apart from my own. My thoughts turned once more to the little Fiat I'd seen and I wondered how the interview with its driver had gone. I assumed that Vinci would have instructed his people to check up on the man's identity and I found myself hoping that this would reveal a deep, dark secret – like the man being a paid assassin, for example. Wouldn't that be good?

And if it didn't turn out to be him? In that case, the only logical assumption was that the murderer was still somewhere here in the Villa Gregory. The question was, who?

13

TUESDAY EVENING

On my way back to my apartment, I heard my name being called and saw Malcolm Derby and Melanie sitting beneath an intricate, wrought-iron rose arbour covered in white blooms. At first sight, it was a warm, romantic setting, but from the body language, I once again got the feeling that all was not well between these two. She was looking far from happy but her face brightened up immediately when she saw Oscar. I followed him across the immaculate lawn towards them and Mr Derby waved me into a seat while my dog did his best to climb onto his wife's lap.

'Welcome back, Chief Inspector, I gather you've been inspecting the cells in the local police station.' His tone was light-hearted but there were deep worry lines around his eyes.

I nodded. 'Slightly less luxurious than Villa Gregory.'

His smile faded. 'Tell me something: in your professional capacity, is it just me or is Inspector Vinci about as much use as a chocolate teapot?'

I had to smile at that. It had been one of my gran's favourite expressions. 'I fear that he's lost sight of the fact that most police work is a collaboration, whether it's with other officers, specialists in Forensics and Ballistics, or just embracing offers of help from unrelated individuals. He sees himself as a one-man band. I told him I was keen to see a resolution to this and offered my services but I'm afraid he turned me down as well.'

'About that: how would you feel about returning to your detective chief inspector persona one more time and trying to get to the bottom of what happened? On his showing so far, I don't trust Inspector Vinci to manage it.' I saw him shoot a cautious glance towards the villa. 'Farmer's death has blighted this week completely, but it's not just this week.' He sounded and looked deeply concerned. 'I was very much hoping to get commitments from the members of the group here so we could move on to the next phase of our new project. Now that's been blown to pieces. Apart from the fact that Farmer potentially represented as much as half of the capital investment we need, it's quite clear – and understandable – that all that the others want to do now is to get the hell out of here and go their separate ways. As soon as Inspector Vinci gives them the go-ahead, I'm sure we won't see them for dust.'

I sympathised with him. I was sure a lot of planning and investment had gone into collecting these potential backers together, and if the whole thing went belly up, it would represent a major setback. However, I felt I should warn him not to expect miracles.

'You've employed me to look after security and I'm more than happy to see what I can dig up. In fact, I've already spoken to a former colleague of mine at Scotland Yard and he's investigating the backgrounds of all the people here at the villa just in case we find a skeleton in one of their cupboards.' No doubt he was wise enough to realise that this would include him and his wife as well, but he made no mention of this as I continued. 'All I would say, though, is that even if Inspector Vinci or I manage to identify the murderer, that's unlikely to change things as far as your other potential investors are concerned. Murder's murder and I can fully understand that their overriding priority would be to get away from here and permanently distance themselves from the investment opportunity you were hoping to give them.'

He nodded ruefully. 'That, of course, is absolutely right. Whatever happens over the next few days, I'm afraid we're going to have to go back to square one and start trying to put together a fresh proposal for another group of willing investors. Piers is glued to the computer as we speak, putting out feelers in the hope of generating interest among people we haven't approached yet.' He gave a frustrated snort. 'Whoever killed Farmer just about killed the whole project.'

As he said this, a thought entered my head. Could it be that whoever had committed or orchestrated Farmer's murder had in fact not necessarily had a grudge against the man himself but had realised that, by taking out the person who would almost certainly have been the major shareholder, the project might well never survive? Could it be that Farmer's murder was in fact simply a piece of cynical commercial skulduggery? I put that idea onto the back burner for now and concentrated on the matter in hand.

'I'll certainly do my best to find out who killed Jonathan Farmer. I understand that Inspector Vinci's in the process of interviewing a man who was seen just a few hours after the murder in a rented car parked not far from here. The back gate was open so it could be he got in and committed the murder, but I'm convinced he could only have done it with the help of somebody inside. If you're sure you want me to get involved, I'm going to need your blessing to sit down and interview each of the guests – including both of you, I'm afraid. I'm sure nobody's going to like it but I'll explain that I'm trying to establish who was where when. Then I'll ask if anybody saw or heard anything or anyone that might help with the investigation. That way, I can draw up a picture of how the murderer might have gained access to Farmer without being seen. Is that all right?'

He nodded. 'No problem. You do what you've got to do.'

'Great. Maybe if you'd be kind enough to tell everybody that you've asked me to do this, they might be more willing to cooperate. Needless to say, if any of them refuse to talk to me, there's nothing I can do about that. The days of DCI Armstrong are long gone now.'

'I'll definitely tell everybody this evening; probably over dinner will be the best time. Will you be joining us? We'll eat at eight.'

'It's very kind of you to ask me but no, thank you. You don't want to be bothered by me.' I stopped and thought about it a bit before changing my mind. 'In fact, thinking about it, it probably *would* be a good idea for me to join you this evening after all. This will allow me to take a closer look at the faces of the people around the table. I've come across quite a few cold-blooded killers in my time and very few of them would have been capable of looking cool, calm and collected only a matter of hours after murdering somebody – especially in such a primitive, barbaric way. Just one thing: I wonder if you'd be good enough to ask Rocky if it might be possible to have a circular table tonight. That way, I'll be able to see everyone's faces. You never know, I might just spot something.' I gave a little shrug. 'It's worth a go. In fact, please could you delay announcing that I'll be questioning people until the end of the meal, in the hope of lulling our killer into a false sense of security? Then, when you speak to them, say that I'll conduct the interviews tomorrow morning. I'll sit down now and prepare a list of names and times for you so that people know when I'd like to see them. Let's say I'll do the interviews in the small lounge. Is that all right?'

He nodded in agreement. 'Sounds good. That's the way we'll play it, Mr Armstrong.' He hesitated. 'Do you mind if I call you Dan? You know I'm Malcolm and this is Melanie. I don't think we need to stand on ceremony, particularly after everything that's happened.'

'Dan's fine, thanks. Now I need to go and take a shower to rinse the old lag smell off me. I'll see you later.'

Oscar and I went back to the apartment where the first thing he did was to make a beeline for his bone and set about it once again. I stripped off and took a shower, emerging feeling a lot better. It had been a crazy day and although I felt it had been a sensible idea to accept Malcolm Derby's offer to eat with the rest of the group this evening, under normal circumstances, I would have been riotously happy just having something light, a quick walk with Oscar, and early to bed. As my ex-wife had often reminded me, I wasn't a twenty-year-old any more.

Dinner was served on the terrace once again. I went over to the villa and put my head around the kitchen door just before eight, keeping my knee firmly in front of Oscar, whose nose was twitching in spite of having spent an hour reducing the already chewed bone to a fraction of its original size. Antonella and Rocky were both in there and they came out to talk to me while Emile remained immersed in his culinary labours.

Antonella even gave me a hug. 'I'm so glad the police realised their mistake and let you out, Dan. I really don't know what that stupid man thinks he's doing: first Rocky and then you.' She lowered her voice. 'Do you really think it was somebody here at the villa who killed that young man?'

Although to my mind the answer to that one was 90 per cent yes, I decided to keep my options open for now. 'It could well be, but there's also the question of whether somebody could have got in through the little gate.'

'But it was bolted, at least it was when I checked on Sunday!' Rocky shook his head decisively. 'And besides, even if somebody had managed to get over the wall or opened the gate, how on earth could they have got into the villa? The downstairs windows were all closed and locked, and there was no damage when I checked this morning. The same applies to the doors.' He glanced at his wife. 'The only way the killer could have got in would have been with the help of somebody here so, even if they didn't actually stab the victim, this means that somebody here is an accessory to murder at the very least.'

I nodded in agreement, heartened by what he'd said. If he or his wife had been persuaded or bribed into allowing access to the killer, this would have been a pretty strange thing to say. Of course, it could be a double bluff, but somehow, I had already pretty well discounted these two along with the chef, just as I had ruled out Malcolm Derby, as potential suspects. After all, Derby had just instructed me to carry out a further investigation, which would have been a strange thing for a murderer to do. I also couldn't see Melanie or Eugenie as killers although I had definitely got the impression last night that neither had liked the victim. My money was on either the Swiss couple, the Canadian oil tycoon, Gus Cornish, Piers, the opera singer – or a hired killer sent by her nefarious husband that she had assisted – or, regretfully, Virginia. I just prayed that it didn't turn out to be her – for her mum's sake and, by extension, for mine.

'I reckon you're right, Rocky. What we've now got to work out is who it might have been. When I was a young detective, I was taught to consider every case from three points of view: did the perpetrator have motive, means and opportunity? In other words, except in those cases of completely random killings, people are almost always killed for a reason – not necessarily a valid reason, of course, but valid in the eyes of the killer. That means there must be somebody here who had the motivation to want Mr Farmer dead. As far as the means of doing it is concerned, any one of us could have picked up one of the knives from the music room and used it to stab him. To work out who might have had the opportunity, tomorrow morning, I'm going to sit down with everybody and see exactly who was where last night. I'll be looking for the one who had the chance to get into Farmer's room, stab him, and get out again unseen, or who might have been able to let the actual murderer in.' They both nodded sagely and I gave them a wave and walked around to the terrace.

I was delighted to find a circular table with eleven place settings. As far as I could see, everybody was already assembled out here on the terrace. Most people hadn't bothered to dress up for the occasion, although Antoine Dujardin's sidekick, Eugenie, appeared wearing a skirt that was little more than a belt, and a tight-fitting top that left very little to the imagination. Fortunately, Oscar, who normally loves the ladies, made no move to go over and greet her, which, considering the length of her skirt and the height above ground level of his cold, wet nose, was probably just as well.

I helped myself to a glass of cold mineral water from a tray on a side table. I wanted to be sure that my mental faculties remained sharp this evening in case one of my dinner companions might say or do something that might incriminate them. As I sipped it, Piers came over to speak to me.

'I heard what happened to you this afternoon. What on earth's going on? Has the inspector gone totally mad? I wonder who he'll arrest next.' It was said in a semi-jocular tone but I felt I could sense real concern beneath his levity. Might this mean that young Piers, beneath his all-black exterior, had something to hide? I shrugged my shoulders.

'I know no more than you do, Piers. Inspector Vinci works in weird and wonderful ways. I understand that there's a detailed post-mortem going at this moment, which might throw up some fresh information but, for now, all I can say with reasonable certainty is that it's still looking to me as though somebody here in the villa either committed the murder or enabled somebody from outside to get in and do it.'

The expression on his face changed from concern to what looked like genuine fear. 'You're saying you still think there's a murderer among us?' His eyes swept across the faces of the others, as did mine, but without identifying any signs of guilt. If our killer really was one of these people, he or she was doing a very good job of remaining inscrutable.

14

TUESDAY EVENING

Rocky arrived to tell us that dinner was served and we all took our places at table. I had toyed with the idea of establishing a seating plan in advance that would give me maximum visibility of the people I considered to be the most likely suspects but, as it worked out, there was no need. I chose a seat with Melanie on my right and Piers on my left. This way, I was able to see the faces of almost all the other guests to some extent and in particular the faces of the Canadian couple, the Swiss couple and Gus Cornish almost full on. Virginia was clearly visible beyond Malcolm to my right, but I couldn't see him full face, and the same applied to Eleanor Leonard, who was on the other side of Piers.

Antonella arrived with the antipasti. Not hors d'oeuvres – antipasti. Clearly, Emile was embracing the fact that he was now in Italy and the result was spectacular. He gave us his own take on bruschetta, adding some slices of bread topped with a delicious seafood mix and some with foie gras and grated truffles, as well as the traditional Tuscan toppings of chopped tomatoes and chicken liver pâté. These were served with a salad of fresh artichoke hearts and a selection of salami and cured ham. As I munched my way through these delights, every now and then passing down a bread-stick to Oscar – mainly to stop him drooling on Melanie's shoes – I surveyed the scene. Was I sitting down to dinner with a killer and, if so, who was it?

Eugenie and Gus were engaged in conversation – well, to be honest he was doing all the talking and she was just nodding occasionally – and they both looked relatively relaxed. Antoine Dujardin spent most of the evening sending and receiving text messages. He appeared stressed, but I didn't know him well enough to be able to tell whether this was normal Antoine or something more. Tonight, Herr Baumgartner – 'call me Erich' – was once again doing his best to drain the European wine lake and he had resumed his jokes and storytelling of the previous night. Maybe it was me being over-critical but I had the feeling that maybe tonight he was a little bit less hearty than before, but I had to remember that less than twenty-four hours earlier, a murder had taken place. Proximity to violent death can knock the stuffing out of anybody. Beside him, his wife, who probably had a first name but who only answered to Frau Baumgartner, sat there and picked at her food, sipped mineral water and occasionally shot acid sideways looks at her husband. This was pretty much what she had been doing the previous evening and I couldn't see any immediate change in her features that might have suggested culpability.

Then there were Eleanor Leonard and Virginia, and both looked deeply troubled. Of course, I told myself, they knew they were in a house where a brutal murder had taken place and they were no doubt both intelligent enough to realise that they were now potentially sitting at table with a killer. Eleanor, or 'Miss Leonard' as Malcolm called her, looked very uncomfortable. It had been a hot day and it was still a warm evening but that didn't completely explain the sweat beading on her forehead. Might there be a more sinister reason for this? As for Virginia, she looked completely zonked. Her face was pale, her eyes red-rimmed and her lovely hair, which had been meticulously styled the previous night, had now just been gathered into a bunch at the back of her head. There was no question about it: she looked bleak.

Of course, I told myself, not only had she slept in a room next to a murder; she had also been close – although at this stage, I didn't know how close – to the victim. It was clear she'd been crying. Was this grief at the loss of a good boss, a lover, or some sort of outpouring of remorse for something she'd done? I was very glad that Anna wasn't here this evening or I felt sure she would have sensed my doubts about her daughter. My relationship with Anna had been going so well, but I was under no illusion that if she were to guess that I was entertaining the possibility of her daughter being a murderer, that wouldn't do much to improve relations between us.

That left me alone with Melanie and Piers. I remembered the way he had appeared attracted to her the previous evening, but I couldn't see how liking his boss's wife could have made him likely to have murdered an unrelated billionaire. As for Melanie, I had pretty much discounted her but I tried to play devil's advocate for a moment. She was an attractive woman and probably very similar in age to the victim. Was it possible that the two of them might have some shared history? What if he had hooked up with her and then discarded her? Would that have provided the motivation for her to kill him? I seriously doubted it, but I decided I had better query to what extent she had known the victim when I interviewed her in the morning.

The starters were followed by a mixed salad with a very French vinaigrette and then turbot in a smooth, blue-cheese sauce accompanied by tiny roast potatoes flavoured with rosemary. I enjoyed every bit of it and was looking forward with keen anticipation to seeing what Emile had prepared as dessert when a voice from across the table stopped me in my tracks.

'Hey, have you guys seen this?' It was Antoine Dujardin, brandishing his phone. 'We're all over the front pages.'

'We're what?' Malcolm Derby sounded as shocked as I was. I was still struggling to work out how on earth the news could have leaked out when he asked the same question that was rattling around in my head. 'How the hell did they find out?' He turned towards me and gave me an interrogative look. 'Any ideas, Dan?'

I took my time before replying. 'I suppose it's possible that Inspector Vinci may have been responsible. He certainly has a very unorthodox style for a detective. If I'd been in his shoes, I wouldn't have said a word to the press until I had at least some concrete leads, and preferably not until I had the perpetrator in custody.' I looked around the table, noting only surprise and concern. Could the news really have been given to the press by Adolfo, the chocolate teapot? Alternatively, could it have come from one of my fellow diners? Surely not. It then occurred to me that there was always the man with the silver Fiat. Maybe the car hadn't belonged to a hired assassin but to a journalist who had somehow got wind of this meeting and had come here looking for a scoop. Well, if that was what he was, it certainly looked as if he'd achieved his aim.

I looked at the faces around the table and read near-universal outrage on them. In particular, Eleanor Leonard looked appalled, and I felt sure that I could also spot fear on her face. Fear of what or of whom? Her husband, maybe. He had a reputation for being reclusive and secretive so seeing his wife's name splashed across the front pages as being involved with, or even a potential suspect in, a murder investigation probably wouldn't go down well over in Greece. Her expression of fear might be at what she expected her husband's reaction to be. Glancing sideways, I caught what might have been a spark of guilt on the face of Piers but, as he was sitting alongside me, I got barely a glimpse before he turned away. Had he maybe been supplementing his salary by selling the information to a contact in the news media?

Dessert was homemade crème caramel, accompanied by handmade little ginger rolls filled with Chantilly cream. My head was still churning with the ramifications of the news having leaked out and I barely tasted it, although I'm sure it must have been wonderful. What seriously concerned me now was that if the villa had been named in the article, there was the very real chance of an international posse of journalists and paparazzi descending on us. By sunrise tomorrow, the sky above us could be filled with drones, filming everything that anybody did here, and the three-metre-high brick walls might not prove to be an insurmountable obstacle.

As soon as I finished my dessert, I made my excuses and stood up, quietly reminding Malcolm to announce the interviews to take place in the morning as soon as I had left the table. After a very quick circuit with Oscar, I went back to the apartment and pulled out my laptop, determined to do something I should have done earlier. Inspector Vinci had told me that the name of the man in the silver car had been Lawrence Butler, and a Google search almost immediately revealed an American journalist of the same name. I clicked onto his Facebook page and realised at once that this had to be our man. He described himself as a freelance investigative journalist and his feed consisted of dozens of newspaper articles bearing his name – some in the US, some Canada, and some in the UK – that had appeared over the last few years. There was no mention of Villa Gregory yet, but he was probably still out celebrating his scoop.

When I checked the front pages of tomorrow's papers, there were stock photographs of Jonathan Farmer on most of them, and inside several of the tabloids, I found a photo of the villa, although I couldn't see it named. I blew it up and studied it closely. As far as I could tell, it had been taken from quite some distance – quite possibly from the top of the boundary wall somewhere around the replica Leaning Tower. I was mildly surprised. Surely, if Butler had managed to get access through the little gate into the grounds, he could have got some far closer shots and, indeed, shots of recognisable faces of people on the terrace. In this photo, all that could be made out were a couple of figures on the terrace, neither of them distinct enough to be recognisable. So what did this mean? Had he maybe not come in through the gate after all? But, if he hadn't, who had? Or, indeed, had it merely been a red herring dreamt up by the real killer?

I gave a frustrated snort and sat back. Oscar looked up from his bone and gave me an inquiring look. I shook my head.

'It's all right, dog, you concentrate on your food.'

Reassured, he returned to the job in hand. As for me, the frustration had not only been brought about by the fact that it was now public knowledge that Farmer had been murdered and that there were a number of big names involved. The other reason for my frustration was because I had been hoping against hope that the owner of the silver Fiat might have had something to do with the murder. It now appeared that this was almost certainly not the case and it was looking ever more likely that the murderer was indeed one of my companions here at the villa. Of course, that wasn't definite. I could remember a character called Jeremy Bent about ten years earlier who had lived up to his name. This self-styled journalist had committed a series of robberies all over London with the sole aim of trying to make it look as if he was brilliant at his job, getting scoop after scoop. We had finally caught him, but it had wasted an awful lot of our time and we had been very happy to see him sent to prison for a number of years as a result.

I was still puzzled about the little gate being open. Unless some more compromising photos appeared over the next twenty-four hours, I was becoming more convinced that the man with the silver Fiat probably hadn't come in that way at all. Had the gate been opened to allow in a hired killer or had it been opened by the real murderer inside, just to muddy the waters of the investigation?

My phone started ringing and I saw that it was Anna. I picked it up and tried to sound cheerful and relaxed – no mean feat after spending an afternoon in a police cell.

'*Ciao, bella*, how's things? I tried to call you earlier but you were otherwise engaged.'

'I've been very busy but I'm fine, but, more importantly, how are things there?'

I gave her a quick summary of the afternoon and evening's events and she sounded duly shocked, particularly when I told her that I had spent a couple of hours in a cell.

'That inspector must be a total moron! How could anybody accuse you of murder?'

'There are murderers everywhere, even in the police, but I'm delighted you don't think I could have done it. I hope your daughter feels the same way.'

'How is she? I've tried to phone her a couple of times this evening, but there was no reply.'

'We were having a group dinner so I expect she left her phone in her room or put it on mute. I would imagine she'll be back in her room by now. Why not try giving her another call?' I didn't want to worry her, but I thought I'd better prepare her for what awaited her. 'She was looking pretty grim this evening, poor thing. Of all the people here, she was the one who knew the guy who was killed best of all, so I'm sure she's still in shock.' I would dearly have liked to ask Anna if she had any idea how close Virginia had been to her boss but I chickened out. As it was, from what her mum said next, it wouldn't have helped much.

'I never met him and she didn't talk about him that much, but from the few comments she's made about him, I didn't like him. She said she thought he was brilliant, but he was very full of himself, an inveterate womaniser, and she thought he might even be doing drugs.'

'I'm afraid the pathologist has confirmed that he had indeed been taking cocaine as well as alcohol last night.' I did my best to strike a reassuring note. 'He was almost certainly unconscious when he was stabbed, so he wouldn't have felt a thing.'

For a moment, it appeared that I had sounded a bit too reassuring. 'Oh, Dan, how can you sound so matter-of-fact about such a barbarous act? It's appalling.'

'I know, I know, I'm sorry, but you can get used to anything over time. Anyway, why don't you give Virginia a call? I'm sure she'd appreciate a bit of support from her mum. Although she and I've exchanged a few words in the course of today, I'm clearly still not flavour of the month with her, or I would have tried to go and comfort her myself. Give her my phone number and tell her that if there's anything she needs or if there's anything she wants to talk about, just to give me a shout. I've promised Mr Derby that I'll do my best to find the perpetrator. Tell her not to worry.'

'I'll do that, but do be careful, Dan. If the murderer really is still there in the villa and knows that you're ferreting about, you might be the next victim.'

I hadn't really considered this as a serious possibility up till now so I mulled it over for a few moments, reluctantly accepting that there was a chance she might be right. I did my best to sound even more reassuring this time when I answered.

'I'll be fine. You know me, Anna: nine lives... like a cat.' I caught Oscar's eye for a moment when he heard the 'C' word, but he soon returned his attention to the remains of the lamb bone.

'Don't joke about these things, Dan. Watch your back.'

'I will, I promise.'

15

TUESDAY LATE EVENING

About twenty minutes later, Oscar suddenly abandoned the remains of the bone and got to his feet. He was starting to walk towards the stairs when I heard a knock on the downstairs door. He hadn't inherited much in the way of a guard-dog gene from his parents, so he just glanced at me as much as to say, *Well, go on, then, answer it.*

I went down the stairs and opened it to find Virginia standing there. I gave her a friendly smile and beckoned to her to come in. Presumably, her mum had convinced her to come to me for help. 'Come in, go on up the stairs. Oscar will be delighted to see you but he's too lazy to bother coming down the stairs to greet you.'

I stood to one side of the little entrance lobby as she came past me and climbed up to the flat. By this time, Oscar had worked out that he was being visited by a woman and his tail was wagging energetically. I followed Virginia up the stairs and found her crouching in the middle of the room making a fuss of my happy Labrador. Determined to keep it light, I pointed towards Oscar.

'If you fondle his ears, he'll be your friend for life. Alternatively, just give him food. That seems to work just as well.' I walked over to the little kitchenette. 'Would you like a drink? I was just going to make myself a cup of tea. It's real English tea. I get it from a place in Florence.'

She looked across at me and I definitely felt I could detect at least a hint of a nervous smile on her face. 'A cup of tea would be great, thanks.'

I busied myself making it while she took a seat on the sofa with Oscar sprawled happily at her feet. I deliberately said nothing and gave her time to settle down. Apart from the upset of the recent murder, I knew it couldn't be easy for her to sit down and drink tea with the man who had, in her eyes, supplanted her father. When it was ready, I took the two cups across and set them on the low coffee table, positioning myself on a chair opposite her so as not to crowd her. I gave it half a minute or so before making an attempt at conversation.

'It's been quite a day, hasn't it?'

She looked up from her tea. 'Mum told me you were locked up for several hours this afternoon. I didn't know... I'm sorry.'

'It all turned out all right in the end.' Still trying to keep it light, I added, 'Besides, it's always good to see the other side of the coin. God knows, I've sent enough people to cells in my time.'

'Did you enjoy being a policeman?'

I was genuinely surprised. This sounded like an attempt to start a conversation. I didn't know what I'd been expecting when I'd opened the door to her, but it hadn't been this. I tried to answer honestly.

'It's a tough job. The hours are brutal and some of the stuff you see as a detective in the murder squad is even more brutal... and senseless. Some very bad people, but so much of the time, the crimes are committed by quite normal people like you and me, who've just been pushed over the edge by force of circumstance.' I saw her nod several times, apparently in agreement, before dropping her eyes back down to the floor, and I felt a sudden sense of foreboding. Could it be that she had come here to unburden herself, maybe even to confess to the murder of her boss? Doing my best to reject that notion – at least for now – I carried on trying to answer her question. 'What is it they say in the movies? "It's a dirty job but somebody's got to do it." It wasn't always a dirty job but, in answer to your question, overall I did enjoy it because I felt I was doing something where I was making a difference. That's important in a job, don't you think?'

She ignored my question and just sat there for a full minute before finally raising her eyes towards me. 'It could have been me.'

I sat and waited for her to say more but she was clearly struggling so I tried a gentle prompt. 'It could have been you what, Virginia? Are you saying you think you could have been the murder victim rather than Jonathan Farmer?'

Her eyes were still trained on my face, but I could tell that her mind was elsewhere. Finally she spoke. 'No, I mean it could have been me who killed him.'

'What makes you say that?' I kept my voice low so as not to disturb her train of thought. I awaited her reply eagerly, taking heart from the fact that it appeared she was indicating that she hadn't committed the murder. But what did she mean? I had to wait some time but she finally started talking again, her eyes now looking somewhere over my left shoulder into the middle distance. It was almost as if she was talking to herself.

'Jon was a monster.' She immediately stopped and corrected herself. 'No, that's not fair; he could be good, kind even, and there's no question that he was probably the most brilliant man I've ever met in my life, but he had a dark side, a very dark side, especially where women or money were concerned.' She paused but I made no comment for now, letting her take her time. After a few seconds, her eyes returned from wherever they had been and caught mine. 'I'm no fool. I knew full well why Jon insisted I come here with him this week. Yes, I speak Italian, but he's been sniffing around me for weeks, months, ever since I started working for him, and I'm sure he saw this as his opportunity to seal the deal.'

'You think he brought you here to have sex with him?'

She nodded. 'Without question, but the message I've been trying to get across to him from the start has been that I'm not interested. I'm sure there are plenty of women out there who would find him attractive, and plenty of women would find his millions *very* attractive, but, like I say, not me.'

'Well, good for you.' I kept my voice low so as not to interrupt her flow. I had a feeling I knew what might be coming next, so I did my best to ease her into it. 'Do you feel like telling me exactly what happened last night?' She made no attempt to reply so I tried again. 'I couldn't help noticing that there was a chair wedged up against the door between his room and yours. Did he try to get into your room?'

This comment clearly surprised her as I saw her eyes widen. 'You saw that?'

She lapsed into silence again, so I added a little bit more ammunition. 'What happened to the top button of your pyjamas? Did you just lose it, or did it get torn off?'

I saw this hit home. 'He did it.' She took a big breath and launched into her tale. 'I went up to my room last night not long after you went off to take Oscar for a walk. I was about to get into bed when there was a knock at the door – the door to the corridor, not the communicating door. I'd already wedged the chair under the handle of that one just in case. I unlocked the door and opened it a little bit so I could peer out and see who it was. It was Jonathan. The next thing I knew, he'd pushed the door wide open, and he came barging in. He was clearly stoned out of his head and there was a really frightening look in his eyes – they were wide, staring.' She was still looking straight at me and, almost for the first time, I read genuine emotion on her face. 'I was scared stiff; I mean terrified, really terrified.'

'I can imagine. And that's what happened to the button?'

She nodded and dropped her eyes to the floor. 'He tried to tear my pyjama jacket open and he scratched me as he lunged at me. I felt sure he was going to rape me...' Her voice tailed off and I could hear the frightened little girl inside this woman's body. Even though she wasn't my daughter, I could feel real anger rising up inside me.

'But he didn't...?'

She shook her head and then looked back up at me, this time with a determined expression that reminded me so forcefully of her mother, I almost stretched out my arms and hugged her. 'No, he damn well didn't. I did a self-defence course at the local gym a couple of years ago and I knew what to do. I disentangled myself from him, stepped back and then kicked him as hard as I could in the groin.' A flicker of satisfaction crossed her face. 'He folded in half and fell forward to his knees, gasping for breath. I grabbed him by his hair and made him crawl along the floor until he was out of my room and then I left him there in the corridor still on all fours, slammed my door and locked it.'

Resisting the urge to catch hold of her hands and squeeze them, I settled for a big smile. 'You're your mother's daughter, all right. Well done you.' I was feeling elated, not just at hearing this story of her resolve and resourcefulness, but also because it was sounding more and more to me as though there was no way she was a murderer. Still, I needed to be sure. 'And did you see him again?'

'No, he didn't try to come back.' Then the expression on her face changed from one of satisfaction to something more stark. 'The thing is, like I said before, the way I felt when he was attacking me, if there had been a knife to hand, I've absolutely no doubt that I would have had no compunction about picking it up and sticking it in him.' Her expression changed to one of horror. 'I could so easily have committed murder. Have you any idea how that made me feel, how that still makes me feel even now?'

I nodded slowly. 'It may surprise you to know that I do, not just because in my police career, I came across far too many cases of assault and murder in circumstances just like that, but because I once found myself in almost exactly the same position.' Now it was my turn to stop and search for my words. It occurred to me that I was about to tell her something known only to one other person in the world: Sergeant Bruno James, my superior officer back then, over thirty years ago. I'd never told anybody else, not even my ex-wife or Anna, but, somehow, I knew I needed to share this with Virginia to help her and, who knows, maybe to help me as well.

'I was still in my mid-twenties, younger than you are now, and it was only my third year in the force. My sergeant and I were called to a domestic incident. Neighbours in a flat on the eighth floor of a tower block in south-east London had called the emergency services because they could hear screams coming from next door. When we got there, there was a little crowd of people outside on the landing and the screams inside were blood-curdling. We kicked the door in and found a drug-crazed man repeatedly beating and stabbing a girl, barely out of her teens. There was blood everywhere, her face was horribly scarred, and you could see she was in agony. I leapt on the guy and wrestled with him for the knife and, just for a moment, when I managed to get him onto his back on the ground and tore the knife away from him, I actually raised it and came very, very close to stabbing the bastard. Before I could do anything, though, my sergeant reached over and gently took the knife out of my hand. If he hadn't done that, I honestly don't know what would have happened.' I repressed a shudder at the memory. 'So, yes, I think I do know how you feel.'

Two things then happened in short succession. First of all, there was a movement at my feet and a big, black paw, followed by a hairy nose, landed on my lap as Oscar realised I was in need of a bit of canine support. Seconds later, Virginia leant forward and caught hold of my hands with both of hers. She gave me a smile, a real, genuine smile this time.

'Thank you, Dan.'

That was all she said, but I knew that a milestone had been passed.

By mutual unspoken agreement, we relapsed into silence while we both drank our tea. Oscar, reassured that he had done his bit, wandered over to the fireplace and resumed his assault on the remains of the lamb bone. When we both felt like talking again, I checked with Virginia in case she had seen or heard anything else in the course of the night, but she was unable to help. What she did say was that it had taken her at least a couple of hours to get to sleep after her ordeal. From what the pathologist had said, this meant that she must have been lying there awake while the murder was committed on the other side of the communicating door, and yet she had heard nothing. Assuming she was telling the truth – and I was now far more convinced that she was – this added further confirmation to the supposition that the victim had been killed while unconscious so there had been no screams, no shouts, no sounds of a struggle.

By the time she left, I was feeling greatly reassured that I'd drawn closer to Anna's gutsy daughter and had been able to remove her from my list of suspects, but I was no nearer finding out the identity of the real killer. As I drifted off to sleep, I found myself reflecting on what Anna had said. Could it be that the murderer would strike again and, if so, might that target really be me?

16

WEDNESDAY MORNING

Wednesday morning dawned bright and clear again. In spite of my fears, I could see no sign of unwelcome journalists at the gates or drones in the skies above and I hoped that would continue. Oscar and I took a slightly longer walk, this time a circuit through the fields beyond the villa walls, and I breathed deeply, reflecting that if I was ever locked up again, I would really miss these walks in the country with my four-legged friend. To my surprise, as I rejoined the road again, a couple of hundred metres or so from the main gates, I saw two police cars emerge from the villa and head off back towards Pisa, blue lights flashing. I hurried in through the gates and saw a lone squad car parked outside the main entrance. I couldn't see anybody to ask so I headed for the kitchen to query what had brought the police back. Rocky opened the door to me and spared me the trouble of asking.

'See the police cars? He's at it again.'

'When you say "he"...?'

'That idiot of an inspector. He and his men turned up here ten minutes ago and they've made another arrest. That makes three now! This time, he was preening himself and strutting around like a cockerel on Viagra.'

This sounded interesting. Maybe the post-mortem had thrown up some significant information. 'And who is it this time?'

His answer left me almost speechless.

'The pretty girl with the dark hair; you know, the assistant to the guy who got killed the other day.'

I could feel myself gawping gormlessly at him. 'He's arrested Virginia? Why on earth would he do a thing like that?'

He shrugged his shoulders. 'Who knows with our friend Adolfo? Maybe the fairies told him, or maybe he's just working through everybody here, one after another. I've just told Antonella she'll probably be next.'

I looked around wildly, my mind racing. What could have made Vinci pounce on Virginia? It had to be something that had emerged in the course of the post-mortem. I gave it some thought and looked back at Rocky as it dawned on me. 'DNA, I bet that's it.'

'You think they found her DNA on Farmer's body?' An expression of surprise crossed his face. 'Do you mean that he and the girl were...?' He gave me the unmistakable Italian gesture with a clenched fist that indicates sexual antics.

I shook my head. 'No, from what she told me last night, she had no interest in him, but she worked closely with him so it's more than feasible that there might have been an eyelash or one of her hairs on him.' Then a thought occurred to me. She had told me he had scratched her when tearing at her pyjama jacket while trying to rape her. I knew that it was standard practice for Forensics to check under the fingernails of victims and presumably they had located and identified some of the skin he had scraped from her body. All it would have needed would have been a minute quantity. The police had taken samples of DNA from all of us here at the villa on Tuesday morning so it would have been simple to find a match.

This was serious. It was self-evident that Virginia had been the best-placed person to have carried out the murder. The communicating door – unlocked on the victim's side – would have given her easy and undetected access to his room. Assuming they had found her DNA on him, that would indicate clearly that Farmer had been in close contact with her, and a court would only have her word for the fact that he had been trying to assault her, rather than the other way round. I could testify that she'd told me her version last night but, in view of my links with her mother, that would carry little weight. For once, it looked as though Inspector Vinci had got all his ducks in a row. Trying to prove that she was innocent was going to be tough and, from the alarm spreading throughout my body, I felt ever more protective towards her. But what could I do?

I thanked Rocky for the information and headed through into the main part of the villa where I almost immediately ran into Sergeant Paola Innocenti.

She gave me a little smile. 'Good morning, *Commissario* Dan. Have you heard that the inspector thinks he's found his murderer?' From the way she said it, I got the feeling she wasn't as convinced as her boss that he'd got it right this time.

'Good morning, yes, Rocky's just given me the news. The problem is that I'm afraid the inspector's got it wrong again. I'm only guessing, but was this morning's arrest because the autopsy revealed DNA evidence underneath the victim's fingernails?'

She looked genuinely surprised – and impressed. 'Yes, traces of skin belonging to Virginia Newton. That's why she's been arrested, but how on earth did you know that?'

I related what Virginia had told me the previous night about the attempted rape and the scratch. 'I believed her. I'd better come clean and disclose now that she's actually the daughter of my girlfriend, so in the eyes of a magistrate, I'm sure I would be considered an unreliable witness, but I genuinely did believe her. The problem for me now is going to be trying to prove her innocence.'

I received a sympathetic smile in return. 'I must confess that I don't see her as a killer either, but the fact of the matter is that the DNA evidence is compelling.'

I caught her eye. 'Well, I don't have much option now. I imagine the inspector has no interest in investigating any further, so I suppose it's down to me to discover the identity of the real murderer.'

'If I can give you any help, I will.' I was heartened that she answered so promptly.

I thought quickly. 'Presumably this means you'll be giving the passports back and allowing people to leave?'

She nodded. 'I'm going to go back to the station in a minute or two and I was planning on coming back with the passports before lunch, just as soon as the inspector has finished interviewing his latest suspect.'

'Is there any way that could be delayed at least until tomorrow? I'm planning to sit down and question all of the main suspects this morning in the hope that I can dig up something. Also, with a bit of luck, I should be hearing from my friend at Scotland Yard in the course of today, so if everybody could be kept here for one more night, I'd be very grateful. Do you think that might be possible?'

I saw her thinking hard. 'The inspector went off a few minutes ago saying that as soon as he's finished interviewing the suspect, he's going out for lunch, followed by a game of golf – that's shorthand for going home for a snooze so I doubt if he'll be back at his desk until tomorrow. He told me to go ahead and return the passports today but he didn't specify a time. What if I were to come around at, say, nine or ten o'clock tonight? I'll still be carrying out his orders, but hopefully by then, it'll be too late for people to make travel plans. I'm afraid that's the best I can do.'

'That's brilliant, thank you. I really appreciate that. Can I ask you one more thing and then I promise I'll let you get on? How did the interview with the American journalist go?'

'Inconclusive, I'm afraid. He freely admitted that he was trying to spy on the people here in the villa but he insisted that he never came into the grounds. He told the inspector he had no idea there was a back gate, and he said all he did was to climb a tree and take some shots over the wall. According to my constable who was in there with them, the inspector threatened him with all sorts and he managed to put the fear of God in the man, but the guy still stuck to his story. Reluctantly, the inspector had to let him go. There's no law against walking in the fields or climbing trees. If anybody in the villa feels strongly enough about him trying to invade their privacy, they'll have to start a civil case. It's outside our domain.'

I nodded. She was right, the investigation was back to square one as far as the journalist was concerned. Of course, it was predictable that he would deny climbing over the wall or coming in through the gate for fear of being charged with trespass or worse, but I tended to believe his story. After all, I had yet to see photographic evidence that he had got any closer to the villa and, if he had known about an open gate, I felt sure a dedicated investigative journalist would have used it and then used the photos. There still remained the question of how he'd heard about the meeting here on Monday night and how he'd discovered the identity of the other players. Clearly, he must have had a contact on the inside, but that didn't mean he'd committed the murder. No doubt he'd come here to spy on a top-level meeting and the discovery of a gory murder to report must have come as a very welcome bonus. Also, how had a journalist from Chicago managed to get here so fast? Presumably, he had already been here in readiness, which made it all the more likely that this spying mission had been pre-planned together with an inside accomplice – but who?

The more I thought about it, I was ever more sure that the open gate would turn out either to be a red herring or the way the real killer had got in and out again – and that hadn't been Lawrence Butler. I thanked Paola Innocenti and she gave me another salute.

'Good luck with your investigation, *Commissario*. If you think I can be of any help, just call me.' She handed me a card with her phone number on it and I thanked her again. After that, I headed out onto the terrace where I found Melanie Derby having break-fast on her own. Oscar got to her first and almost made her spill her cornflakes as he tried to climb onto her lap. I followed behind quickly.

'Oscar, leave the lady alone.'

She looked up from petting the Labrador. 'Hi, Dan, don't worry about Oscar, he's lovely. Have you heard about Virginia? I can hardly believe it. On Monday night, Piers and I were really quite worried about what Jonathan Farmer might be planning to do to her. Farmer was completely wasted, so at least I suppose it'll be treated as self-defence.'

I adopted a confident look that I didn't really feel. It would be Virginia's word against the inspector's. 'Yes, I would hope so, but I'm not convinced she did it.'

'You aren't?'

She looked genuinely surprised, and I couldn't help noticing how her overall demeanour had changed over the last twenty-four hours. When I'd first seen her, I had sensed that all might not be well in her marriage, but the death of Farmer appeared to have shocked her to the core. Was this just a natural reaction to the death of another human being or was there more to it than that?

Her voice stirred me from my thoughts. 'If not Virginia, then who could it have been, and why? Why, Dan?'

'That's what I've been trying to figure out and, hopefully, this morning's interviews with everybody will help me get a clearer picture. Tell me, how well did you know Farmer? On Monday night, I definitely got the feeling that you didn't like him.'

'To be perfectly honest, I thought he was a reprehensible human being.'

'You knew him well, then?'

'I knew *of* him.' She looked up and caught my eye. 'We were both up at Oxford at the same time and even back then, he had a frightful reputation.'

'In what way?'

'He was a cheat!' That was real strength in her words. 'He cheated at everything: his studies, his relationships and at cards. Apparently, he and a group of others played poker for ridiculously high stakes, and nobody could beat him. They all knew he was cheating but they couldn't prove it. I heard of people losing thousands. One guy even tried to take his own life and, although it was never proved, the talk around the college was that it had been down to gambling with Farmer.'

'You say you knew *of* him; was that as close as you got to him?'

I saw her shudder. 'Yes, thank God. One of my friends went out with him a few times and he treated her appallingly. No, I'm delighted to say I had no personal contact with him.' She looked up at me again. 'The funny thing is that I almost feel sorry for him now he's dead. He was a horrible man but nobody deserves to die like that, do they?'

'Good morning, Dan.' A voice from behind me made me turn my head and I saw Gus Cornish emerge through the French windows, looking as suave as ever in immaculately ironed, grey, linen slacks and a lemon-yellow polo shirt. He came over to where

I was standing. 'In view of the latest developments, I presume there's no need for you to question everybody this morning after all.'

I shook my head. 'No, I'd like to stick to the plan. The inspector's arrested Virginia, but I think he's got the wrong person yet again.'

For a moment, his air of bonhomie slipped and an expression of annoyance – or more – crossed his face. 'Surely you can't be serious. The inspector said they had watertight DNA evidence. "Watertight", that's what he said.'

All of a sudden, I saw Augustus Cornish in a new light. Beneath the veneer of smooth socialite, I had just glimpsed something less amiable. Why, I wondered, was he reacting like this? Was it just because he didn't want his guests to be troubled any more, or might this mean that he had something to hide? He was already on my list of prime suspects and I resolved to make sure I grilled him as thoroughly as I could when we met later on.

Deciding to leave them to their breakfast, I persuaded Oscar to abandon his lady friend and as I was leaving, I addressed Cornish again.

'I'm just going back to my apartment now to prepare for the interviews. I seem to remember that you're the first? See you at ten. Okay?'

He looked anything but okay, but he gave a reluctant nod.

When I got back to my flat, the first thing I did was to phone Anna but, predictably, it went to voicemail as she was almost certainly in the classroom. Rather than leave her a message telling her that her only daughter had just been arrested for murder, I asked her to call me back when she had a moment. As far as Virginia was concerned, I was increasingly worried and I felt unusually helpless, knowing there was little I could do. She was in a cell, I couldn't even go and see her as we weren't related, and I had a murder to solve. As far as I could see, it was now up to me to find the real perpetrator because Adolfo Vinci appeared to have washed his hands of the affair.

I stood there for a few moments with my phone in my hand, wondering whether to call Virgilio in the hope that he could intercede on her behalf, but I hesitated. As the sergeant had said, the evidence against Virginia was strong and I didn't want to cause trouble for my friend if this was a lost cause and she turned out to be guilty. But could she really have done it? When she had left my apartment the previous night, I had been convinced of her innocence but I knew it wasn't going to be easy to prove. In the end, all I could do was call Lina, explain the circumstances, and ask her to get hold of a good lawyer in Pisa and send them along to the police station to represent Virginia's interests.

The phone started ringing, but it wasn't Anna. It was Paul at Scotland Yard and he'd been as good as his word, getting his people to investigate my companions here at the villa, producing some interesting results.

'I think I might have two or three leads for you, Dan. In fact, I might have more leads than you need or want. Let's start with the guy behind the meetings. Malcolm Derby appears on the face of it to be a successful businessman who's risen through the ranks to head up this new company as part of the Grunstock empire. However, my people tell me it's not quite what it seems. Apparently, he's been moved sideways into this new company after a serious sexual harassment scandal involving one of the female members of staff in the previous place. The word on the street is that a considerable sum in hush money was paid to her, much to the displeasure of old man Grunstock, and, as a result, this is last chance saloon for Derby.'

This was interesting. It also went a long way towards explaining why his wife had not looked too happy with him.

However, as far as I was concerned, this would make it even more improbable that he might have wanted to kill his major investor. I would have to look into this carefully all the same. 'Brilliant, Paul, that could be really useful. Anything on his wife? She told me she was at university with the victim.'

'Nothing, I'm afraid. She married Derby three years ago and, as far as we know, she's a happy housewife. No occupation listed.'

'Any kids?'

There was a pause while he checked his records. 'Nope, none.'

'What about the Swiss couple? Have you been able to find out anything about them?'

'Nothing of any use to you. I'm afraid trying to get information out of the finance and banking world is notoriously difficult, and it gets many times more difficult when you throw Liechtenstein into the equation. There are more finance houses registered there than you can shake a stick at, and my colleagues at the Serious Fraud Office tell me that tracing ownership often leads to a tangled web of offshore companies. Baumgartner's company is called Mauren Investments and they're a major international player. All I can tell you is that Erich Baumgartner is sixty-one while his wife, Birgit, is seventy. Nothing shady as far as my people can find out but, I repeat, we don't have very much information on them. I'll ask my people to keep digging, but I'm not optimistic.'

This meant that jovial, budding alcoholic Erich Baumgartner was Frau Baumgartner's trophy husband and I found myself smiling. Surely she could have done a bit better for herself if she'd been looking for a toyboy, but maybe it had been his money that had attracted her. Alternatively, remembering a constant criticism my ex-wife used to make of me, maybe it had been a love match after all, and I was just a cynical old copper. But, either way, I couldn't see that either of them had a motive for murdering Jonathan Farmer.

Meanwhile, Paul was continuing with his report. 'The Canadian couple aren't a couple.'

'So it's just a business arrangement, is it?'

I heard him chuckle. 'Definitely business, but not the oil extraction business. Eugenie Laroche is a call girl based in Montreal, Canada. It would appear that Antoine Dujardin has just brought her along for the ride, so to speak.'

'Well, well, well, that explains a lot. I think she'll definitely merit further investigation. Thanks a lot for that. What about Antoine Dujardin himself, anything on him?'

'Nothing shady on file. His family is one of the richest on the planet and, as the only son and current CEO of the family business, he stands to inherit the whole shebang one of these days. That leads us on to Eleanor Leonard, the opera singer, and this is where it gets more interesting. She recently married a billionaire Greek almost three times her age and, guess what, I wouldn't mind betting it was the attraction of his money, because she hasn't got any.'

'But surely she must have made millions in the course of her career?'

'She did, but it's gone. It's all very hush-hush, but a journalist friend of mine tells me it appears that she invested the lot in a dodgy investment fund that promised amazing returns but came crashing down, taking all her savings with it. She lost everything.'

'Mmm, I wonder who was behind that scheme? Anna's daughter, who worked for Farmer, told me that he had a dark side when it came to women and finance. If it turns out he was behind that scam, then suddenly the opera singer has considerable motive for committing murder.'

'I'll go back to my contact and see if he can find out more about the company involved. By the way, you'll be pleased to know that we couldn't dig up anything negative about your

Virginia Newton or about Derby's assistant, Piers Cooper-Stevenson.'

'Thanks a lot, Paul.' I was checking the names off on my notepad. 'And the guy who owns this place, Augustus Cornish? Any dirt there?'

'Nothing we could find. He inherited the place from his father and he has a reputation as a bit of a playboy, but he appears to be inoffensive.'

'Any previous connection with the victim?'

'Not so far as I can see. That's all I've been able to find out for now but I'll keep my ear to the ground. What's the state of play over there now? Any closer to finding the killer?'

I gave him a brief rundown of the latest developments and he sounded very sympathetic. 'This Inspector Vinci sounds like a right prat. Surely you don't believe that Virginia's involved in murder, do you?'

'No, of course I don't.' But I found myself turning it over in my head yet again. My instincts were telling me she couldn't have been involved but, as the sergeant had said, the DNA evidence was compelling and she had had the best opportunity and the motive of self-defence. Yes, she'd told me what had happened in her room, including the scratch he'd inflicted on her, but that might have just been an intricate bit of dissimulation. I could well imagine the horror on her mother's face if she had been able to read my mind so, steadfastly trying to remain positive, I thanked Paul most warmly for his help and rang off.

As I started to think in detail about this morning's interviews, I reflected on what I'd just been told. Paul was right: he'd furnished me with information that might well produce motives for murder in a number of the people I was about to sit down and talk to. There was the glamorous opera singer, maybe out for revenge after losing her money in a financial scam, possibly orchestrated by the victim. There was the Canadian call girl and a big question mark over her relationship with Antoine Dujardin. Had she just been brought along by him for a bit of light relief, or had she come with a more sinister purpose? I remembered what Gus Cornish had said that first night about there being some dodgy people in the group, so maybe there might be a skeleton in the cupboards of the Swiss couple or even Malcolm Derby, desperate to redeem himself in the eyes of the all-powerful Alexander Grunstock.

I had a feeling this morning's meetings were going to be illuminating.

17

WEDNESDAY MORNING

The interview with Gus Cornish took place in what was called the small lounge – which was twice the size of my own living room – at ten o'clock as agreed, but it didn't last long. I started by asking him what he'd meant when he'd mentioned that not all of the participants in this week's meetings had the best of reputations. He gave me a grim smile.

'There's no need for me to tell you about Farmer, I'm sure. You don't get to be that rich that quickly without being unbelievably lucky or being prepared to sail very close to the wind. I'm sure there are quite a few people around the world smiling this morning as they pick up their newspapers and read that he's been murdered. A bright guy, but with the moral fibre of a slug.'

'I take it from that that you didn't like him.'

He caught my eye. 'I didn't know him well, but the little I did know I didn't like, but that doesn't mean I murdered him.'

'Of course; now what about the others? What about the Swiss couple?'

'As far as I'm aware, Erich and Birgit's operation is legit, but the word on the street is that they have some very shady clients.'

'Are we talking money laundering?'

'I really couldn't say for sure, but I wouldn't be surprised. Last night, Erich was pissed again – God, he can put the booze away – and he was boasting about how his company deals with the rulers of half the countries in Africa. I don't know if that's true or not, but it wouldn't surprise me.'

'Does Eleanor Leonard fall into the suspicious category?'

He shook his head. 'I'm sure *she's* fine, but her husband, old man Aristotelis, has definitely got a few dark secrets.'

'Such as?'

'Gun running or whatever it's called these days. I've spoken to people who're convinced his ships are being used to take arms to some of the nastiest regimes in the world. They just can't prove it.'

'Might that have been your friend the Italian Minister of Justice, for example, who told you that?'

All I got back from him was an enigmatic smile, so I moved on. 'What about Antoine Dujardin? Did you know him before?'

'I've known Antoine for a good long while and he's okay. I definitely wouldn't include him in the dodgy category. Not least because his dad would never countenance anything illegal. The Dujardin family is one of the best known in Canada and they're pillars of the Montreal community. They're also heavily into the Catholic Church, and they've apparently had audiences with two different popes. That's why I'm sure Antoine's clean.' He glanced over his shoulder even though the door was closed and the room was empty. 'Although I'm seriously concerned about his taste in women. Eugenie's drop-dead gorgeous, but could you see her being introduced to the Pope? She'd probably give the old boy a heart attack.'

I had to smile but I made no comment. 'And Malcolm Derby, you know him quite well, don't you? Piers told me that Malcolm was here for your Christmas party.'

'Malcolm and I were at school together. We've been friends since we were in short trousers, locked up in a Jesuit boarding school in Yorkshire. He'd hardly spent any of his life in England up till then and at the age of seven it must have been even tougher for him than it was for me. I think he's got problems in his business life and also in his private life, but you'd need to ask him about that.'

'And what about you, Gus? How do you fit into all this? You say you didn't know Farmer well?'

'Only by reputation. As for how I fit in, I'm doing Malcolm a favour by letting him use the villa at a knockdown price but apart from that, like I told you, I'm just the landlord.'

'Have you any suspicions as to who might have killed Farmer?'

'You still don't believe it was Virginia, then? Personally, I'd be prepared to put money on it being her, but I'm not saying it would have been murder. Most probably manslaughter or whatever it's called when you're trying to defend yourself from assault. I think we could all see what Farmer had in mind on Monday night and I feel sorry for the girl, but if her DNA's all over him, then it's pretty incriminating, isn't it? If it wasn't her, then I really don't know.'

'Finally, please can you tell me your movements on Monday night?'

'After dinner, I went down to the pool with Eugenie and Antoine, but then I just went back up to my apartment and went to bed.'

'Can anybody confirm that? Eugenie, maybe?'

He shook his head. 'No, she just went off to her room.'

And that was all I could get out of him.

The next on my list was Eleanor Leonard. It didn't take me very long to discover that she was terrified of her husband. Apparently, he had already seen the headlines and, by the look on her face, he hadn't been best pleased. I gently brought her around to the subject of her financial difficulties and she looked shocked.

'You know about that?'

I didn't really know very much about it at all, but I nodded and hoped that she would elaborate. With a little bit of prompting, she finally told me what I'd been suspecting.

'My husband sent me here in response to an invitation from Alexander Grunstock – they know each other pretty well. He's started using me as his ambassador.' I couldn't miss the bitter note in her voice. Clearly, marriage to an elderly billionaire came with a number of downsides. 'My job was to listen and then report back. I had no idea who the other investors in this new project were likely to be and when I saw Jonathan Farmer walk in, I came very close to leaving the villa there and then.'

'Because...?' I kept my voice low and gentle.

'Because he's the swine who swindled me out of my money.' She looked up from her hands, straight at me, a pleading expression on her face. 'I know how this must look to you, but I promise you I didn't kill him. I can't say I'm sorry he's dead but, at the same time, that doesn't get me my money back.' She shook her head sadly. 'Because of him, my whole life has been turned upside down. I hated him for doing that, but I couldn't prove it. He had companies owned by other companies owned by shady offshore operations. I got lawyers looking into it but every trail just ended up in a dead end and then the last of my money ran out. But you must believe me, there's no way I would ever contemplate murder.'

And presumably when her money finally ran out, that was when the Greek billionaire came along. I changed the subject. 'Tell me, is it possible that the Baumgartners' company might have been involved in the same scam that lost you your money?'

She shook her head. 'I really don't know but I doubt it. From what my husband tells me, they're a highly successful company with a lot of financial expertise. I'm sure they would never have let themselves be hoodwinked like I was. Besides, by the sound of it, their opinion of Farmer was even lower than mine.'

'Why was that? Are you sure Farmer didn't screw them as well?'

'I could believe anything of Farmer but I would imagine Erich would have steered clear of him. You'd better ask him or his wife.' Her expression darkened. 'She's a tough character; maybe she's the real killer. I could imagine her being capable of anything.'

I knew what she meant, but of course just having an unwelcoming demeanour didn't necessarily make the Swiss woman a killer.

I saw Miss Leonard look at her watch. 'Is that all you want to know?'

'Yes, thank you, I appreciate your honesty. One more thing: did you go straight to bed after dinner on Monday and did you see or hear anything suspicious?'

'Yes, I went straight up and no, I didn't see or hear anybody. I just went into my room and locked the door. I didn't like the way Jonathan Farmer was looking at me.'

Just before she reached the door, I asked her the same question I was asking everybody. 'One last thing: if Virginia didn't kill Farmer, and if you didn't kill him, can you think of anybody here at the villa who might have done it?'

She just shook her head mutely and reached for the door handle.

My next interviewee was Eugenie. Today, she was wearing short shorts that looked as if they'd been sprayed on. Oscar, who had probably been dreaming about food or squirrels, looked up with interest as she came in and I waved an admonitory finger at him to stay where he was. A cold Labrador nose in the posterior probably wouldn't have improved her mood, and it was patently already far from good. She ignored my gesture to take a seat and stood in front of me, hands on hips.

'You realise you have no authority to question me. You're not the police and, besides, I've done nothing wrong.'

I nodded in agreement. 'You're quite right, Eugenie, I have no right to question you, and if you prefer not to say anything, that's completely up to you. But before you go off, maybe you could just satisfy my curiosity first. I used to be in the Metropolitan Police and I asked a friend of mine over there to run your name through the computer. He's just called me to tell me that you aren't employed by Antoine Dujardin's company as we thought, although there may be a business arrangement of a different kind between the two of you. Can you just tell me if that's correct?'

She had already been heading for the door, but I saw her stop. She stood there with her back to me for a few moments before I saw her shoulders drop and she turned and came back to take a seat on the chair I'd indicated earlier. 'So what if I'm here in a different role? That's strictly between Antoine and me.' She was putting on a pretty defiant act and I could see I was dealing with a tough cookie, but I could also detect a distinct trace of anxiety in her voice.

I nodded my head. 'Of course it is, but I'm interested to know why he chose you as his companion.'

'That's nothing to do with you.' She was still acting tough, but I'd dealt with tougher characters than this one before.

'Fine, if you don't want to tell me, I'll just pass the information on to the inspector. You may find he has a more aggressive way of questioning.'

She stared at me for several seconds before she gave a resigned nod of the head. 'Antoine and I've known each other for almost two years now. He's been good to me and he sometimes takes me with him when he goes on trips.'

'Thank you.'

Of course, she was quite right. Whatever arrangement there was between the two of them had nothing to do with me and, more importantly, almost certainly had nothing to do with the murder of Jonathan Farmer. So why was there this edge of anxiety in her voice and in her eyes? I had a sudden moment of inspiration and took a chance.

'And what about you and Lawrence Butler, the journalist? What's your connection with him?'

She was a good actor, and no doubt that was a prerequisite in her chosen career, but she still couldn't hide the spark of shock and guilt that flitted across her face for a fraction of a second before she dropped her eyes and answered. 'Lawrence who? I don't believe I know anybody called Lawrence.'

I leant forward towards her and lowered my voice. 'Listen, Eugenie, I know you're the person who tipped off the journalist about this meeting and then about Farmer's murder, and I'm quite sure Antoine will take a very dim view of it if I tell him.' I waited until she looked up from her hands and made sure she could see the determination on my face. 'I said *if* I tell him. This can remain between you and me, but I need to know everything. No bullshit, just the truth. It's your decision.' I sat back and waited while she was clearly considering her options. Finally, she made a decision and I heaved a silent sigh of relief.

'Larry – that's Lawrence – and I have worked together for three years now. I feed him bits of information that I get from my clients, and he sees that my rent gets paid.'

'Are you saying that as soon as you were invited along this week, you told him who was going to be here, and he came along to spy on them?'

She shook her head. 'Pretty much, but I didn't know all the names until I got here. In fact, Antoine didn't either. When he saw that Farmer guy out on the terrace on Monday night, I thought he was going to have a fit. I don't know the background, but I know that there's bad blood there.' Realising what she had said, she suddenly stopped and wagged a manicured finger in front of my face. 'Don't get me wrong. I'm not saying Antoine had anything to do with the murder. He wouldn't hurt a fly.'

'You're sure of that?'

There was a brief pause before she answered. 'Listen, this is strictly between you and me, okay? Antoine couldn't have killed Farmer because he was otherwise engaged on Monday night.'

'In what way?'

'Antoine and Gus wanted me to go with them for a swim and, afterwards, when I went to bed, I know the two of them went up to Gus's apartment. I went into Antoine's room on Tuesday morning and his bed hadn't been slept in.'

'Antoine and Gus...? Are you saying?' Considering I had over thirty years of police work under my belt, I gave myself a mental kicking. Surely I should have noticed something. After all, the pink tux should have given me a clue. I listened in awe as Eugenie continued.

'The deal I have going with Antoine is a smokescreen. He takes me places just to keep his folks happy. They're hardcore religious freaks and they would disown him and, more importantly, disinherit him, if they knew he was gay. Like I say, that's why I'm here, as a façade. I like him a lot and it's easy money.' For a moment, a hint of a smile crossed her face. 'I had you fooled, as well, didn't I? I'm good, you know.'

She really was. I promised her I wouldn't reveal her secret and she went off looking happier than before. As the door closed behind her, I found myself wondering why Gus Cornish hadn't told me the truth about what had happened on Monday night. Natural shyness, or something more sinister? Had he and Antoine Dujardin clubbed together to murder Farmer?

The plot was thickening.

18

WEDNESDAY LATE MORNING

My interviews with Piers and Melanie were quickly over. Piers kept telling me how he couldn't believe that Virginia could have committed the murder, and he sounded genuinely concerned for her. No, he hadn't seen or heard anything suspicious, and after a short session with Malcolm, he'd gone straight back to his room, but then had spent two hours on the computer working for his boss before finally crashing out around 1 a.m. As for Melanie, when I saw her, I didn't bring up the question of her husband's sexual harassment case and just started with basic questions, which resulted in nothing new. Although I felt confident that she'd told me the truth before, I tried to find out a bit more about what had happened at Oxford years ago.

'You mentioned a student who played cards with Farmer and lost so much that he attempted suicide. Can you remember the guy's name?'

She had to stop and think but it came back to her. 'Ed... Edward Smythe. He was doing a PhD in Classics. I remember hearing that he came from a posh family, but I don't think they had a lot of money. That's why, when he lost so much, he spiralled into acute depression.'

'Have you kept in contact with him since then?'

She shook her head. 'To be honest, I hardly knew him then. I think I heard that he got a job in a university up country somewhere, but I'm afraid I don't know any more than that.'

'And your girlfriend who went out with Farmer, but was badly treated by him?'

'Lottie Mackenzie. Yes, I'm still in touch with her and we meet up once or twice a year when she comes to London. She lives in Edinburgh with her husband and three children.'

'You have no children of your own?'

She shook her head again. 'Alas, no. We wanted kids, we still do, but it just hasn't happened.'

Finally, I asked her about Monday night and she told me she hadn't heard or seen anything suspicious and had gone up to bed after dinner. She had been joined shortly afterwards by her husband, who had been tidying up a few loose ends downstairs.

That, of course, meant that Malcolm had been on his own for several minutes during which he could conceivably have committed the crime but, once again, I couldn't see the logic of his killing the goose that laid the golden eggs. Farmer had potentially been his principal investor after all. Even so, when I got Malcolm in, I asked him to repeat exactly what he'd done on Monday night and his story corresponded to what Piers and his wife had said. The slight delay between Melanie going to bed and him following her had been because he'd been discussing Tuesday's programme with Piers. As a result, I felt fairly confident – although still not 100 per cent – that I could rule all three of them out of my investigation.

He was followed by Antoine Dujardin who repeated what Eugenie had said about their late-night swim, after which all three had returned to the villa. I asked him if anybody could confirm where he had spent the night and he shook his head.

'I just crashed out. I'd probably had a bit too much to drink.'

I looked him square in the eye. 'I don't like it when people lie to me in a murder investigation, Mr Dujardin.' He bridled but made no comment. From what Eugenie had said, I knew he was lying to prevent word of his sexual orientation getting back to his parents, potentially with cataclysmic effects on his future prospects, but if he could lie about this, he could lie about more serious matters as well – like murder. 'I'm going to ask you again Mr Dujardin, can anybody vouch for where you were on Monday night?' I didn't want to drop Eugenie in it, so I improvised. 'You see, I happened to notice on Tuesday morning that your bed hadn't been slept in.'

A look of shock, almost immediately followed by contrition, appeared on his face. 'You're right. I didn't spend the night in my room. I was with Eugenie.'

I didn't like the way he was still lying – assuming I could believe Eugenie – so I decided to up the ante. 'That's not what Gus Cornish told me.' I saw his cheeks flush and I hastened to reassure him. 'How you live your life is no concern of mine and I promise that anything you tell me will remain between the two of us. I'm trying to get to the bottom of who committed a horrible murder and if you carry on lying to me, the finger of suspicion is going to point all the more directly at you.' I saw this hit home and I gave him one more push in the right direction. 'I'll ask you once again: can anybody vouch for where you spent Monday night?'

He hung his head and I felt sorry for the guy. In this day and age, it seemed archaic and particularly cruel of his parents to insist that he be something he wasn't. When he spoke, he sounded crest-fallen – and scared. 'Yes, I spent the night with Gus and there's no way I could ever kill another human being, even a scumbag like Farmer.' He looked up and there was a pleading expression on his face. 'You said that this could remain between the two of us, didn't you? I have very strong personal reasons for wanting to keep my relationship with Gus a closely guarded secret.'

I nodded. 'Of course, your secret's safe with me. Like I say, I'm trying to catch a murderer, nothing more.'

My words appeared to reassure him, and he gave me an enquiring look. 'You don't think Virginia did it, do you?'

'No, I don't. Tell me, if she didn't do it, and you didn't do it, and Gus didn't do it, have you any ideas as to who might have done it?'

He shook his head slowly. 'Farmer was a very successful man, but he didn't always play by the rules.' He then went on to say almost exactly what Gus Cornish had said before. 'I'm sure there are a lot of people out there who are very happy to read of his death. However, hating him so deeply that they would resort to murder is a different matter. I really don't know. What I can tell you is that I disliked him intensely, but I didn't kill him.'

'Thank you, that's all for now.'

This left me with the Swiss couple, scheduled to come and talk to me at eleven o'clock. Eleven came and went and there was no sign of them. I gave it another ten minutes and then went out to look for them. I found Frau Baumgartner sitting in the lounge, sipping peppermint tea. When I asked her if she would come with me to the other room, her answer was predictably monosyllabic.

'No.'

'It would really help me in trying to find out who killed Jonathan Farmer. I won't take much of your time.'

She gave a haughty shake of the head. 'The police have already arrested the culprit. I see no reason why I should let you poke your nose into our affairs.'

I was trying to think of a better way of convincing her when I was interrupted by noise in the corridor outside, and the door was flung open to reveal Inspector Vinci, with a face like thunder.

Oscar, who had been snoozing quietly in front of the empty fire-place, looked up with an indignant expression on his face. The inspector marched across to me and jabbed me roughly in the chest. I don't like people poking me and I had to fight the urge to reach out and break his finger.

With difficulty, I produced a cordial expression and tried to sound placatory. 'Good morning, Inspector. How's your investigation going?'

'There *is* no investigation. The investigation is closed. I have arrested the perpetrator and that's that. What I want to know is why you are so clearly disobeying my instructions and seem to be trying to carry out some sort of parallel investigation that you have no authority to do.'

I wondered who'd told him about this. I could see Sergeant Innocenti standing by the door behind him looking impassive but it would have surprised me if the news had come from her. A few seconds later, the identity of the source was revealed when the inspector turned towards Frau Baumgartner and gave what might have been almost a hint of a bow.

'Thank you, Signora Baumgartner, for your call. I don't like it when people try to set themselves up as amateur detectives.'

Frau Baumgartner even managed to strain her face muscles sufficiently to form an approximation of a smile. 'Thank you for coming so quickly, Inspector. My husband and I appreciate your concern.'

What was interesting was that she was speaking to him in fluent Italian, albeit with a noticeable Germanic accent. Up till now, I had had no inkling that she spoke the language. I had no more time for reflection as the inspector's pudgy finger jabbed me yet again in the chest.

'There are to be no more questions. The guests here are free to leave. You, in particular, would do well to take your smelly mutt and leave Pisa as soon as possible before I lock you up again. Is... that... clear?'

Between each of the last three words he jabbed me again, and I have to confess that I came very close to giving him a clout. As it was, my faithful canine companion suddenly rediscovered his guard-dog gene, came up behind the inspector and produced a marvellous, cavernous, echoing woof. The inspector jumped as if he'd got the fright of his life and whirled round, levelling a kick in the direction of the Labrador. Oscar sidestepped the blow as neatly as a matador, the big man lost his balance and tumbled to the floor. As he hit the ground, there was the unmistakable sound of a shot. There was stunned silence for several seconds and then Adolfo Vinci screamed in agony after which, mercifully, he fainted.

He had shot himself in the foot.

Frau Baumgartner leapt to her feet and distanced herself from the stricken detective and the blood that was spurting out of his ankle. I dropped to my knees alongside him and took a closer look. From the quantity of blood coming out, it looked as though the bullet must have severed a serious artery. First things first, I reached into his jacket and gingerly removed the massive pistol from the holster under his left armpit. There were still wisps of blue smoke coming out of the end of the long barrel as I very carefully placed it on the floor out of harm's way. Turning my attention to the wound, I pulled up Vinci's trouser leg, removed his shoe and sock and saw that the powerful bullet had done a frightening amount of damage. I looked up towards the door and saw Sergeant Innocenti heading my way, eyes wide in disbelief. I held up my hand.

'This is going to need a tourniquet, Sergeant. I'll do it while you call the emergency services, all right?'

'Yes, *Commissario*.' She turned and hurried out of the door.

I tore off my belt and wrapped it around the inspector's calf, pulled it as tight as I could and secured it. As I did so, I looked up at Frau Baumgartner, who was standing there, her eyes trained on the widening puddle of blood on the floor. 'Please go and find Antonella or Rocky. Ask them to bring a towel.' She didn't move, her eyes still staring fixedly at the stricken detective, so I raised my voice. 'Frau Baumgartner, a towel. Now!'

The message finally sank in and she went over to the door and disappeared.

19

WEDNESDAY LUNCHTIME

I stood on the steps by the front door alongside Sergeant Innocenti and watched the flashing blue lights of the ambulance disappear along the drive. It had been an eventful morning. According to the paramedics, the bullet had struck Vinci's shin at an angle, fracturing several bones on its way, and had managed to sever both the anterior and the posterior tibial arteries. My improvised tourniquet had met with their approval and, according to them, had probably saved the inspector's life. I rather hoped somebody would tell him that. It might get him off my back.

I glanced sideways at Paola Innocenti. 'What happens now? Do you take over?'

She nodded. 'I've contacted the station and they've told me that as we already have a suspect in custody, they won't appoint another senior officer to the case, and I've been given instructions just to wind things up here.' She glanced over her shoulder but there was nobody listening. 'So what would you like me to do, *Commissario*?'

I gave her a smile. 'Please just call me Dan. Well, as it's now your case, what would you suggest we do?'

'How did your interviews go this morning? Any progress?'

I also checked over my shoulder to see if we were being over-heard and then pointed towards the garden, just to be on the safe side. 'I'm sure Oscar could do with a quick walk. Why don't we go and get a little bit of fresh air?'

We walked down the steps onto the parking area and followed a gravel path that wound its way between clumps of colourful pink and red oleander bushes, bordered by carefully trimmed, low box hedges, before emerging onto the lawn. When we reached the little rose arbour, we sat down on the bench and I gave her a rundown of this morning's interview results and she scribbled in her note-book. When I reached the end, I had to confess that I still had no firm leads.

'I'm going to need to take a bit of time and do some serious thinking, but I'm still convinced that the killer has to be somebody I've spoken to this morning. I just need to work on it. Hopefully, in the course of this afternoon, I should be able to piece together what I believe to have happened. Are you okay to stick with the plan of waiting until tonight to give them back their passports?' She nodded and I continued, really just thinking aloud. 'To my mind, the most likely suspects are Eleanor Leonard, Gus Cornish, Antoine Dujardin and his girlfriend or the Baumgartners.'

I went on to tell her how I'd been unable to interview the Swiss couple because of their refusal to cooperate. Paola now demon-strated that she had a decisive streak.

'*You* may not have jurisdiction to question them, but I do. It's almost lunchtime. They'll probably be in the dining room or on the terrace. Let's go and talk to them now. What do you want to know?'

I told her I was interested to know the exact relationship between them and the victim and whether it was true that they hadn't got on with him. If so, I was interested to know why. Paola

nodded and we headed back to the villa. As expected, we found
most of the guests in the dining room, preferring to stay in the
shade rather than venture out in the heat of the noonday sun. The
Swiss couple were standing in a corner talking quietly and I
followed Sergeant Innocenti across to them. I had omitted to tell
her that Frau Baumgartner spoke pretty good Italian so Paola
addressed them in her pretty reasonable English.

'I have a few more questions for you. They won't take long but
they are important.'

I saw the two Swiss exchange glances and Frau Baumgartner
attempted to object, but the sergeant overruled her. 'If you would
come with me, please, *signora*, we'll start with you.' Without giving
the husband a chance to intervene, she guided Frau Baumgartner
out of the door, along the corridor and into the small lounge. I
followed and closed the door behind us, watching with interest as
Paola sat down on an armchair and indicated the one opposite her.
'Sit down, please.' Frau Baumgartner made no move so, in the face
of this obvious resistance, Paola turned to me, switching back to
Italian.

'Signor Armstrong, I'd be grateful if you would translate for
me. Tell the lady we can either do this here or I can arrest her for
refusing to cooperate with a murder investigation and take her
back to the station where we'll do it in an interview room. Tell her
it's all the same to me. It's her choice.'

Repressing a smile, I produced the translation and Frau Baumgartner, with visible ill will, finally sat down as requested. I took up
position on the piano stool over to one side of them and Oscar
slumped down at my feet as Paola managed to produce a remarkably convincing smile.

'Your name is Birgit Baumgartner and you live in Wollishofen,
Switzerland?'

The answer came back in Italian. 'That's correct, and there's no need for you to struggle with your schoolgirl English or for you to use the services of this gentleman.' The way she said the word 'gentleman' made clear that she didn't consider me to be anything of the sort. 'I lived and worked for twenty years in Lugano so we can do this in Italian, particularly if it speeds things up.'

I was impressed to see Paola rise above the thinly veiled insult and get in a cheap shot of her own for both of us as she switched to Italian. 'You are seventy years old and so, technically, a pensioner. Do you still work full-time?'

If looks could kill, Paola would have dissolved into dust on the spot, but she stood firm and went up even higher in my estimation. Grudgingly, the older woman nodded.

'I work full time in a very responsible job.'

Paola acknowledged the remark and continued. 'When we spoke yesterday morning, you told me that after dinner on Monday, you went straight to bed without seeing or hearing anybody or anything suspicious. Is that still correct?'

'Yes.' The Swiss woman's tone was decidedly icy.

'And your husband was with you and he can confirm that?'

'Yes.'

'I'm interested to know how well you knew Jonathan Farmer. Did you have business dealings with him?'

'No.' Still chilly.

'What about on a personal level? Had you met him before coming here this week?'

'Yes, briefly, but only once.'

'Under what circumstances?'

'I met him at an international financial forum in New York three years ago. I probably only exchanged a dozen words with him in total.'

'I've been told that relations between you and him were poor. Is that correct?'

She shook her head. 'No, whoever told you that was wrong. My husband and I barely knew the man and certainly not well enough to either like him or dislike him.'

I decided to make absolutely sure. 'You're telling us you had no business relations and no close contact with Farmer?'

She gave me the sort of look normally reserved for something picked up on the sole of a shoe. 'I'm talking to the sergeant, not to you.'

Paola gave her an even friendlier smile. 'For my sake, could you just confirm that one more time?'

The woman snorted and stood up. 'I stand by what I've told you. Now, unless you can think of any other pointless questions, can I take it that we've finished?'

'Yes and thank you for your cooperation. Please would you ask your husband to come in now?'

Frau Baumgartner stalked stiffly out of the room and, out of curiosity, I followed her at a discreet distance. When she reached the dining room, I peered through the crack of the door and saw her head straight for her husband. She spent almost a minute speaking to him intently sotto voce and I wondered what that was all about.

When he broke away from his wife and came towards the door, I ducked back out of sight and hurried along the corridor into the lounge. When I got there, I turned so that I was holding the door open in readiness for his arrival. He gave me a cheerful smile when he saw me and did the same to the sergeant when he saw her. Unlike his wife, he appeared only too happy to cooperate – although my old copper antennae told me there was apprehension just below the affable veneer.

He gave the sergeant a sympathetic look. 'I was so sorry to hear about the inspector. My wife and I hope his injury isn't too serious. Do, please, give him my very best wishes for a speedy recovery.' I was pretty sure Paola had understood but I rattled off a quick translation all the same. Erich was positively exuding affability and Paola smiled at him in return.

'Of course I will and thank you for your concern. Do sit down, please.'

The contrast between him and his wife was stark and I wondered, not for the first time, what had brought the two of them together – love, money or something else? He took a seat and sat back, crossing his legs. He looked as if he could have been settling down for an evening on the sofa watching the TV but, nevertheless, I could still sense tension in him. Mind you, that might just have been because he was being interviewed in connection with a murder.

'Your name is Erich Baumgartner and you live with your wife, Birgit, in Wollishofen, Switzerland?' She spoke in Italian and I translated her questions and his replies.

He nodded. 'We're fortunate enough to have a house over-looking the lake. I don't know if you're familiar with the *Zürichsee*, but it's very beautiful.'

'I'm sure it must be. Tell me, please, how long have you been married?'

'Just over fifteen happy years, I'm pleased to say.' As I trans-lated, I had to stifle my incredulity that living with that dragon could possibly be described as happy, but I had to admit that he sounded genuine. If he was acting, he was pretty damn good.

'You told me yesterday morning that when you retired to bed after dinner on Monday night, you heard and saw nothing unusual. Is that correct or have you remembered anything since?'

He gave her a self-deprecating smile. 'To be perfectly honest, Sergeant, I'm afraid I had a bit too much to drink on Monday night, and I don't really remember very much apart from just going back to my room with Birgit and crashing out.'

'Thank you. Now I'd like to ask you about the victim. Did you know Jonathan Farmer?'

'I only met him once, briefly, at a thing in New York, two or three years ago. So, no, I can't say I knew him.'

'Did you ever have any business dealings with him or his company?'

For a moment, a flicker of something crossed his face – distaste certainly but maybe there was more below the surface. 'No, although I didn't know *him* particularly well, his company, or should I say his empire, had a distinctly dubious reputation. We're a reputable firm and we don't work with people like that.'

After a couple more innocuous questions, the sergeant dismissed him and he left, still smiling and repeating unctuous good wishes for the speedy recovery of Inspector Vinci. I waited until the door had closed behind him before catching the sergeant's eye.

'What did you think of our Erich?'

'Slimy.' She used the Italian word, *viscido*, which describes the trail that a snail leaves behind it. 'If I wanted honest financial advice, I'd probably go to your dog before I'd go to him.'

I nodded in agreement. 'Absolutely, but do we believe he might be our murderer?'

'Whoever stabbed Farmer did it very precisely and very clinically, piercing the heart straight away. If Baumgartner was as drunk as he says, I think that would have been unlikely.'

I nodded in agreement. 'As far as I could see, he and Farmer were both equally drunk that night, so he's probably telling the truth.' At that moment, my phone started ringing and I saw that it was Anna. 'I'm sorry, Paola, but I need to take this. It's my girlfriend, the mother of the woman your inspector has locked up.'

Paola gave me a sympathetic smile and I answered the call.

'*Ciao*, Anna.'

'*Ciao*, Dan, what's up? You left me a message to call you.' She sounded happy enough... for now.

I took a deep breath and did my best to break the news to her as gently as possible that her only child was currently being held by the Pisa police under suspicion of murder. Understandably, Anna was appalled and panic-stricken. After a lot of explaining and as much consolation as I could muster, including telling her that I had arranged to send Virginia a lawyer, I agreed to meet her off the train at Pisa Centrale station at five past three. I checked with Paola to see whether it might be possible for Anna to speak to her daughter then, and she confirmed that she would make the arrangements. At the end of the call, I looked across at Paola, who glanced at her watch and smiled ruefully.

'Unless there's anything else you think needs doing here, I'd better get back to the station. I'll see Virginia Newton and tell her that her mother's on the way and that the inspector's no longer on the case. I'm also going to sit down and talk to some of my colleagues and have a serious think about things. Hopefully, between us, we'll be able to establish the true identity of the killer.' She caught my eye for a moment. 'I sincerely hope we can make a breakthrough because there's some powerful evidence pointing towards Virginia Newton being the guilty party. If you're bringing her mother to the *questura* this afternoon, why don't you leave her to talk to her daughter and come up and see me in my office? We can go through everything together one more time. Is there anything else you can think of?'

I nodded slowly. 'A couple of things, if you or your colleagues can find the time. First things first, I imagine the inspector checked to see who inherits Farmer's empire.'

To my amazement, Paola shook her head. 'I suggested to the inspector yesterday morning that we should look into that but, to the best of my knowledge, he didn't bother. He was convinced he had already cracked the case and saw no point in "wasting police time". Those were his exact words.'

I raised my eyes to the heavens. 'How on earth has he managed to last so long in his job?'

I saw her take another cautious look around. 'You're not the only one who has friends in high places. His father was the mayor of Pisa for almost ten years until his death last year. Complaints – and there have been any number of them – were always deflected or other officers got the blame.' She lowered her voice. 'I passed my exams last year to be promoted to inspector but, because I do most of his work for him, he's always kept me as a sergeant.'

I gave her a grin. 'I'm surprised you didn't consider shooting him in the foot yourself.'

She grinned back. 'Don't think I didn't – and not just in the foot. Anyway, checking the will is top of my list when I get back to the station. What else do you need to know?'

'I wonder if you could check whether Dujardin or the Baumgartners ever had financial dealings with the victim. They both claim they didn't, but if there's any way your people can look into both of them a bit more closely, I'd be grateful.'

'I'll see what we can do. Is that it?' I nodded and she gave me another salute. '*Arrivederci*, Dan.'

I thanked her warmly for all her help and reflected after she'd left that if she'd been in charge of the investigation from the start, rather than the would-be Dirty Harry, we might have already cracked the case by now. I checked the time on my watch. It was just after twelve-thirty. In ten hours' time, all of the suspects were going to be given back their travel documents and I had little doubt the first thing they would do would be to use them to distance themselves from this place as quickly as they could.

Ten hours to solve a murder...

20

___

WEDNESDAY AFTERNOON

By three o'clock, I had had time to do a lot of thinking. I had deliberately avoided joining the others for lunch and had settled for a sandwich in my apartment and it was good to be able to sit down in peace and quiet and reflect on the week's events... so far. My main concern was to establish a motive for the murder. In my experience, two of the prime motivators, time and time again, turn out either to be money or sex. Could it be that Farmer was murdered by a jealous woman or a jealous husband or partner? Alternatively, had he been killed because of financial misdoings? His reputation as a womaniser and a ruthless businessman made either scenario equally possible.

Of course, there are other motives for murder. For centuries, people have regularly been killed in duels arising from something as little as a perceived minor insult, and people are still killed every day around the world for their religion, race, political beliefs or their sexual orientation. People get killed because they've witnessed something they shouldn't have seen, and revenge has often been a powerful motive, as well as envy or even ambition. It occurred to me that Piers looked like an ambitious character, so had he maybe realised that by killing the major investor in his boss's new project, he might well be able to torpedo the scheme, and quite possibly that would result in Malcolm Derby losing his job? However, the chances of a twenty-something being promoted to CEO of an important company struck me as cloud cuckoo land so I dismissed that theory.

I felt sure that many thousands of people around the world would have envied Farmer his millions, but the majority of the people here at the villa this week had more than enough money of their own not to have to resort to murder. I wondered about the will. Virginia had told me Farmer had been unmarried and without a serious partner, so who was going to inherit all his money? It would be very interesting to hear, but would we get the information before everybody left the villa?

I decided to leave Oscar with Antonella rather than take him into the hot and crowded centre of Pisa and I left him sitting in the kitchen alongside her with a happy look of gastronomic anticipation on his face. I hoped she wouldn't give him too much to eat or he would probably burst.

Getting into town was easy enough and I managed to find a short-stay parking space directly opposite the station, which was swarming with tourists of all nationalities, locals and the usual selection of less salubrious characters that gravitate around railway stations. With a hand on my wallet just in case, I went in to wait for Anna and was pleased to find that her train arrived bang on time. I had just got to the platform when it came in and she ran towards me when she saw me. I caught her in my arms and hugged her tight. She was obviously in a state of high emotion and I did my best to offer reassurance. She didn't start crying, but I could see that it was a close run thing. When we separated, I picked up her overnight bag and we walked down the steps to the passage beneath the lines and up again into the main concourse.

From there, we went outside and set off across the forecourt to the car.

I immediately went into supportive mode. 'The good news is that the bungling inspector has been replaced by somebody a whole lot more efficient, and I'm confident that between us, we'll be able to get to the bottom of what happened.'

'But is Virginia still locked up?'

'Yes, for now, but hopefully not for much longer.'

Anna knew me well enough by now to pick up on my slight hesitation. She squeezed my arm and pulled me to a sudden halt in the middle of the road, staring me fixedly in the eye. 'She's innocent, Dan, you do believe that, don't you?'

'Of course I do. Nobody in your family could be a murderer.' I grabbed her arm and hurried her across to the pavement. 'Apart from you, possibly. That bus driver almost had to do an emergency stop to avoid us and he gave us both a dirty look.'

'Don't joke about it, Dan, I need to know that you believe in her.'

'I honestly believe she didn't do it, but it's not down to me. The unfortunate fact of the matter is that the DNA evidence is just about the only evidence in this case so far and it's not in her favour. That's why the police are keeping her in custody. Try not to worry and tell her to try to stay positive. When we get to the *questura*, while you're talking to Virginia, I've arranged to meet up with the officer who's taken over the investigation and I'm convinced that she believes her to be innocent as well.'

We set off in the van, crossing the River Arno and heading into ever narrower streets in the direction of the *centro storico*. There were no parking spaces to be found close to the *questura* and I had to drive almost as far as the Piazza dei Miracoli to find a spot. After a bit of a struggle, I managed to squeeze the big vehicle into a tight space between a German-registered Mercedes and a French

Citroën and we walked back to the police station. I was pleased to find that we were expected, and an officer led Anna away to see her daughter while I was directed upstairs to the first floor. Sergeant Innocenti had installed herself in the office with *Ispettore A Vinci* on the door. The door itself was open and Paola waved me in as soon as she saw me.

'Come in and take a seat, Dan. Has your girlfriend gone to see her daughter?'

'Yes, thanks for arranging that. Any developments?'

'No new information yet. We've contacted Farmer's company lawyers and have put in a request to see details of his will, but you know what it's like with these big law firms; they may well take their time. The firm is actually based in Los Angeles, so they're probably only getting out of bed around now. If we're lucky, we might hear something in the middle of the night over here. As far as the financial affairs of the Canadian and the Swiss couple are concerned, nothing to report yet, except that the investigation is being handled by experts from the *Guardia di Finanza* in Rome as a matter of urgency.'

'So we just have to wait.'

'Afraid so. What about you? Did you manage to sit down and think it through?'

'I've certainly been doing a lot of thinking, but without any great success so far; at least, nothing more than a bit of elimination. The more I think about it, the more convinced I am that this was an inside job, so I'm concentrating on the people in the villa rather than a random hitman from outside. To my mind, the open gate was most probably a red herring to divert attention from the real culprit. I feel I can be confident in scrubbing Rocky and Antonella from the list of suspects and I'm reasonably sure that Mr and Mrs Derby and their assistant, Piers Cooper-Stevenson, had nothing to do with it, although I wouldn't completely rule them out. Melanie Derby told me she was at university with Farmer, and who knows the truth of what happened back then?'

'But that must be at least ten or fifteen years ago. Surely it's highly unlikely that she should suddenly decide to take action now?'

'Exactly. I can't see how she could be the killer either, but let's just keep her, her husband and Piers on the list with a question mark alongside them for now. I got the impression that Piers has a soft spot for Melanie so maybe she got him to do her dirty work for her, but I doubt it. I don't believe Eleanor Leonard, the opera singer, is capable of murder, but it's pretty clear that her husband over in Greece moves in fairly murky circles, so I suppose it's just possible that he instructed her to enable a hired killer to come in and do it. Of course, if that is what happened, it's fraught with problems, not least how did she know that there was a back gate, considering it was very well hidden behind all those bushes? When I did my initial recce of the garden from the inside, I didn't spot it and I was looking for exactly that sort of thing. That implies a degree of local knowledge. And with a dozen people wandering about late on Monday night, I find it hard to believe that an unknown person could have sneaked in and sneaked out again unobserved.'

She nodded in agreement. 'That's the way I see it as well. Let's leave Eleanor Leonard on the list but with a question mark alongside her name. Realistically, that gate was only known to the staff or the owner, so that means Augustus Cornish, if we're excluding Antonella and Rocky.'

A thought occurred to me. 'Malcolm Derby and his wife were here at Christmas when there would have been fewer leaves on the trees and bushes. Maybe they saw the gate then and hatched the plan but I've no idea why.' I couldn't stifle a snort of frustration and she gave a wry laugh.

'One step forward and two steps back. Anyway, that leaves us with the Canadian couple and the Swiss couple. Along with Cornish, that makes a total of five prime suspects, all with opportunity and means, and four other less likely suspects. We badly need a motive, but the bad news is that we may not hear back from the victim's lawyers or from the financial people until late tonight or quite possibly tomorrow and by that time, they will almost certainly have returned to wherever they came from.' She shrugged helplessly. 'Of course, we can still keep investigating even if they've left, but it will make it all the more difficult for us.'

I was pleased to hear that the sergeant was thinking along exactly the same lines as I was and shared my desire to resolve matters in a hurry. Just then, another thought struck me. 'Given that Gus Cornish and Antoine Dujardin are in some sort of relationship, I suppose it's possible Antoine killed Farmer, and then Cornish slipped out and opened the gate to throw us off the track. Alternatively, it was a professional hit arranged by the Canadian, and Cornish opened the gate to let the killer in.' I looked across the desk at her and gave her a rueful smile. 'So many possibles, but no definite motive.'

'Apart from Virginia Newton, the woman we have in custody, who has already told us she was assaulted by the victim – and she has a slight scar to prove it – although she maintains she acted in self-defence and only kicked him. By the way, I got the pathologist to check and he confirmed that the victim's groin area exhibited some bruising, although that doesn't let her off yet.' She shrugged. 'I know that isn't what you want to hear but it's the truth.'

I nodded. 'Yes, of course I understand and thanks for double-checking her story. I'm grateful to you for being prepared to entertain the idea that she might be innocent, even though your inspector appears to have no doubts.'

'I also have the feeling she isn't guilty, but, until we can find proof to the contrary, that's all it is: a feeling.'

'How is Inspector Vinci? Any word from the hospital?'

'Two badly shattered bones – the bullet that struck him made a hell of a mess of his ankle – and they're going to have to keep him in for quite a while. To be honest, it's lucky nobody else was hurt. After going through his leg, the bullet from that bazooka of his carried on and punched a hole clean through the base of the solid wooden door before lodging in the wall of the corridor. By the way, the surgeon who operated on him agreed that your tourniquet saved the inspector's life. The leg's going to have to be immobilised from the knee down for quite a few weeks, and they say they won't know for some time whether there's going to be any lasting damage.'

'I was afraid of that when I saw the wound. Why on earth he carried the sort of weapon that can fire bullets through doors is beyond me. I hope he'll consider a change of sidearm as a result of this. At least this'll give you a few weeks to run things here and show your superiors what they're missing by keeping you as a sergeant.'

She smiled. 'If I can start by resolving the Villa Gregory case, I'll be happy.'

'As far as that's concerned, the only solution I've come up with is that we need to try to shake things up a bit. I've been trying to think of some way we could encourage the killer or killers to show their hand.'

'Yes, but how? So far, they've done very well at hiding their tracks.'

'Indeed, so what we need is to dream up a scenario that will scare them into taking action.'

'What sort of action?'

I found myself thinking of Anna's warning to me the previous night. 'The feeling amongst most of the people I interviewed this morning is that the inspector has done his job and you've got the right person locked up. As far as they're concerned, the only person who's still investigating is me, and they can't understand why. I suppose the best thing I can do to shake the killer out of the woodwork is to come up with a means of convincing him or her that the only way to escape prosecution is to eliminate me.'

'You realise what you're saying?' Paola sounded genuinely concerned for me. 'You're saying you're thinking of putting your life on the line in order to flush out the real perpetrator?' She shook her head slowly. 'There's already been one murder at Villa Gregory, Dan; the last thing either of us needs is another.'

'I couldn't agree more – especially if it were to be me – but I'm finding it hard to come up with an alternative plan. I'll go and think on it now and I'll give you a call later on, as and when anything comes to me.' I glanced at my watch and stood up. 'Time's up for Anna's visit to Virginia. I'd better go downstairs and meet her. As I'm sure you can imagine, she's in a terrible state.'

She nodded sympathetically. 'I certainly can. No mother ever wants to think that her child could be accused of doing such a horrible thing, but, of course, all murders are committed by some mother's son or daughter. Let's hope we can come up with something or get some fresh information before tonight. I'll keep thinking as well and, if I don't hear from you, I'm afraid I will have to come along at ten o'clock to return the travel documents to everybody.'

We shook hands and I left her office determined to do everything I could to prove Virginia's innocence, but would I really have to put my life on the line?

21

WEDNESDAY AFTERNOON

I found Anna waiting outside on the pavement, a damp tissue in her hand, looking distraught. We walked back to the van in near silence and I spotted a gelateria a bit further along the road with tables outside on the pavement. A few minutes later, the two of us were sitting under a parasol barely a stone's throw from the Leaning Tower – the real one, not the Villa Gregory imitation – with two of the biggest ice-cream sundaes I had ever seen in my life in front of us. I launched gently into conversation.

'How was Virginia? Did the lawyer see her?'

She nodded. 'She said he was very kind and she told me to thank you for arranging it.'

'But he couldn't get her out?'

'He said that'll be down to a judge, but he warned that because she's a foreign resident, it's unlikely they'll grant bail.' For a moment, I thought she was going to start crying again, but she managed to control herself. I gave it a few moments and then attempted to offer more reassurance.

'Well, I'm going to do my best to ensure that we get everything sorted out before she even has to appear before a judge. Is she terribly upset?'

Anna looked up, red-eyed, from her still-empty spoon. 'I'm not sure if "upset" is the right word. She's obviously very worried and scared, but she's also furious, not so much with the police, although she has a very low opinion of the inspector who shot himself, but of the way Jonathan Farmer is still managing to hassle her even after his death.'

I very nearly asked why, if Virginia had disliked her boss so much, she hadn't just left his employ, but that wouldn't have helped and probably would have spoiled enjoyment of the ice-cream sundaes for both of us. What was done was done, and we needed to move on. I took a mouthful of peach and white-chocolate ice cream, cleverly skewering half a glacé cherry on the end of the spoon as I did so, and savoured it before saying anything else. It was excellent and I encouraged Anna to try hers, which she finally did, but without any outward sign of enjoyment. Clearly food was not high on her agenda for now and I could well understand. I tried to imagine what it would feel like if my own daughter were in the same position. It was scary.

After another couple of refreshing mouthfuls, I returned to the matter in hand. 'What I need to do now is to sit down and think of a way to flush out the real perpetrator before everybody heads off home tomorrow morning.'

She looked up. 'Why don't you talk it through with me? I'd be fascinated to hear all about the villa and the people there and, you never know, talking about it to somebody fresh might help.'

I gave her a little smile. 'Talking to somebody with a good brain like yours is definitely a sensible idea.' I looked around at the nearby tables and thought it best to be discreet. 'Finish your ice cream and let's walk up to the Piazza dei Miracoli. A miracle would come in very handy at the moment.'

As we approached the historic heart of the city, the narrow access road became steadily fuller and fuller of pedestrians as tourists from all over the globe gravitated towards the Leaning Tower. In the square by the main gates in the massive city walls, I lost count of all the different shops and stalls selling souvenirs ranging from the sublime to the ridiculous. T-shirts with the Leaning Tower on them were one thing, but a plastic Galileo – Pisa's most famous son – that lit up and played tunes was a different matter entirely.

Finally, we reached our goal and walked into the broad, grassy expanse of the Piazza dei Miracoli, absolutely swarming with humanity. Ahead of us was the real Leaning Tower, spectacularly tall and leaning at an impossible angle, its white marble exterior gleaming in the bright, spring sunshine and, beyond it, the stunning, circular, marble-clad baptistery and the impressive bulk of the duomo.

As we walked around, I couldn't help reflecting on the contrast between the outstanding beauty of this place of such antiquity and the sordid end of a less than admirable human being only a couple of kilometres away at Villa Gregory. Murder's never pretty, but in a city of such overwhelming beauty, it appeared even more squalid.

I gave Anna a detailed breakdown of the different people at the villa, along with my suspicions. She threw in one or two little queries as I went along but otherwise made no comment until I'd finished. When I finally came to the end of my exposé, she took her time before passing judgement.

'I can see why the police think it was Virginia.' I was relieved to hear her voice sounding almost matter-of-fact. 'Until you get the information about the victim's will and his financial dealings – which should all have been done twenty-four hours ago by the bungling inspector – there really is very little evidence apart from her DNA being found under Farmer's nails. I can also see the problem of trying to keep the suspects at the villa any longer than tomorrow morning, so I agree that this gives you very little time. What are you planning on doing this evening to, as you say, flush the killer out?'

'This is where I'd welcome your input. Any suggestions? Let's start with the hundred-thousand-dollar question: who do you think did it?'

'I really don't know. Either the Swiss or the Canadian if they were cheated by Farmer. The owner of the villa has been lying to you so far so maybe he has something else to hide. Without meeting them, it's hard, but I wouldn't discount any of the women either. The opera singer obviously hated him, and the woman – what's her name, Melanie? – who was at university with him and claimed that he treated women badly might in fact have been badly treated by him herself and she was just pretending when she said that it happened to a friend of hers. The Swiss woman sounds like a real old bat, but that doesn't necessarily make her a murderer. As for the call girl, she demonstrably doesn't share most people's moral compass so it's possible she might have been prepared, if not to commit murder, at least to open the gate and let the real murderer in.'

'But how did she know the gate was there?'

'Yes, that's a point, but I still think she might have done it as, indeed, might any of the others. Basically, unless some spectacular new evidence arrives, you only have one choice.'

'And that is?'

'You've got to frighten the murderer into revealing himself... or herself.'

I nodded in agreement. 'That's the conclusion I've come to as well, but the question is, how? I could announce at dinner tonight that I've found some new evidence and say that I'm going to hand it over to the police in the morning, hoping that the murderer will try to eliminate me and the new evidence. We lay a trap and make sure the police catch them in the act – preferably before they succeed. The problem is that nobody's going to believe for a moment that I would sit on something as explosive as that overnight.'

'Could you have dinner with them, and right at the end, suddenly jump to your feet in a eureka moment and run off to your room, telling everybody you think you've cracked it?' From her tone, it was clear she wasn't convinced. And I wasn't either.

I shook my head slowly. 'Is that any more credible? We have to give the killer credit for being able to see through something like that.'

'No, you're right. I suppose it's a non-starter, really.' By this time, we were on the far side of the duomo, walking close to the imposing city walls. Anna stopped in a welcome piece of shade and rested back against the cool stone for almost a minute before coming up with a suggestion. 'Divide and rule: you've got to engineer things this evening so that each of your suspects thinks you're onto them. From what we've been saying, that could be almost any of them, but I suppose the Swiss man or maybe even his wife, the Canadian with or without the call girl, and the owner of the villa, Mr Cornish, are the prime suspects. Rather than making some sort of an announcement to the dinner table at large, you need to come up with a way of dropping a hint to each of them individually so that they feel they have to take action.'

'That's pretty much what I've been thinking. It isn't going to be easy, but I need to arrange for each of them to hear me saying something or see me doing something that they can interpret as a direct threat but without my making it too obvious. I can't just go up to each of them one by one and say, "I'm pretty sure you're the killer and I'll know definitely in a few hours' time." It's got to be more subtle than that.' I smiled at her. 'Easier said than done.'

Anna didn't smile back. 'And then, presumably, you just sit back and wait for the murderer to try to kill you to shut you up.' She shot me an incredulous look. 'I know you take your job very seriously, Dan, but isn't this maybe going a bit too far, even for you? The murderer's proved to be very efficient. What happens if they find a way of killing you too?'

'Point taken. As you say, it would be very annoying to find myself dead.' I tried to laugh it off, but the expression of concern on her face didn't shift so I returned to more serious matters. 'I have absolutely no intention of getting myself killed so what I need to do, after sowing the seeds in the head of the murderer, is to come up with a trap. I'll sit down with Sergeant Innocenti and make sure she and her people will be lying in wait, ready to pounce.'

'As long as the murderer takes the bait and walks into the trap.' She was looking very worried by now. 'What if they're clever enough to see through the charade and catch you unawares? They've done pretty well up to now.'

'I'll just have to make quite sure that they don't.' I reached over and caught hold of her hand, giving it a reassuring squeeze. 'Don't worry, I'll have Oscar to look after me.'

She shook her head. 'I know he loves you dearly – as do I – but what if the murderer turns up with a *bistecca alla Fiorentina*? I know Oscar's your best friend, but we both know his appetite. Given the choice of good food or protecting a human...?'

I squeezed her hand again and adopted a relaxed air that I didn't really feel. 'He knows where his priorities lie. He'll watch my back.'

Anna still didn't look convinced. 'I don't need to be back in Florence until the day after tomorrow so I'll come back to the villa with you and stay. Two pairs of eyes are better than one.'

The last thing I wanted was for anything to happen to Anna so

I shook my head and thought of a diplomatic way out. 'That's very sweet of you, but it'll be safer for me if you aren't around.' Seeing the incomprehension on her face, I did my best to explain. 'If I'm on my own, I only have to worry about *me*. If you're there with me, however much you want to help, part of me is going to be worrying about what might happen to you, and I might take my eye off the ball. No, thanks for the offer, but the best thing is for you to take a hotel room near the police station and be ready to rush in and give your daughter the good news when the trap has been sprung. I'll call you straight away when I have news.'

Needless to say, this didn't satisfy her and it took me a while before I finally managed to get grudging acceptance from her that it was better for me to work alone, under the hopefully watchful eyes of the police and my dog – steak or no steak.

We carried on talking until I realised that I was going to have to make a move before I got a parking fine. As we walked back to the van, she called a little hotel she knew and, fortunately, they had a room for her. We drove straight there, and I dropped her off by the front entrance. Unwilling to get out of the vehicle, she reached across and grabbed hold of my upper arm with both of her hands and pulled me towards her so that our faces were barely a few inches apart.

'Promise me you'll take care, Dan. Like I said, this killer has proved to be very resourceful so far and I don't know what I'd do if something happened to you.' I could see tears glistening in her eyes and I was desperately trying to think of something reassuring to say when she leant forward and kissed me hard on the lips before drawing back, tears now running down her cheeks. 'The job isn't worth getting killed for, Dan. I love you so very dearly and the idea of losing you is too awful for words.'

I reached over with my free hand and wiped the tears from her face. 'I'll be careful, I promise, but I owe it to you and I owe it to

Virginia to sort this affair out and clear her name. Try not to worry. I'll call you just as soon as it's been done.'

She was still looking anything but convinced, but she finally opened the door and climbed out. Without a word, she turned away and walked resolutely into the hotel, but I could tell from her shoulders that she had started crying again. I knew how she felt. I wasn't going to start crying, but I knew I'd be lying if I'd said I wasn't seriously worried about how the next few hours were going to pan out.

22

WEDNESDAY EARLY EVENING

After leaving Anna at the hotel, I drove back to the villa and collected Oscar from the kitchen. What he and I both needed was a long walk; in my case, to give me time to consider my options for tonight and in his case, in the hope of working off at least some of the calories he had packed down in the last forty-eight hours. We turned left out of the main gate and walked past where I had seen the silver Fiat until we reached the edge of the dense pine forest of the regional park. As we made our way into the trees along a sandy track, I advised him repeatedly to watch out for poisonous snakes, but I wasn't convinced that he understood the severity of the situation. In consequence, I did my best to ensure that we stayed on or near the track and when he brought me sticks or pine cones and dropped them at my feet, I made sure I threw them along the track for him to retrieve rather than into the shadowy undergrowth. Luckily, we didn't come across any squirrels or I knew he would have disappeared into the undergrowth to give chase, regardless of what might be lurking beneath his paws.

All the time, I was thinking about the best way of scaring the murderer into taking precipitous action tonight. I ticked off the

names in my head yet again and gradually began to formulate a
series of situations involving each of the individuals that would
allow me to drop some veiled hints. Although the wall of pine trees
on both sides sheltered us from the direct sunlight, the air was still
very warm and I was sweating profusely by the time we reached a
crossroads where forestry tracks led off in no fewer than five
different directions. Today, with the bright sunshine, it was easy to
keep my bearings by reference to the sun and the direction of the
shadows, but I could imagine that on a grey winter's day, it would
be very easy to get lost out here. Considering we were so close to a
sizable city, it was remarkable to be in such a remote environment.
It didn't escape my attention that this would be a perfect location
for a murder and I made a mental note not to come back here until
the murderer at the villa had been caught.

After a walk lasting well over an hour, Oscar and I returned to
the villa and the first thing he did was to drink a whole bowl full of
water while I stood under a tepid shower and gradually cooled
down. Refreshed and changed, I returned to the living room and
sat down with a bottle of cold mineral water and my notepad and
pencil. While Oscar sprawled at my feet, snoring happily, I slowly
and deliberately sketched out my plans until I had got them as
clear in my mind as I could.

When I was satisfied that I had come up with the best possible
solution, I called Sergeant Innocenti. She listened intently to what
I had to say and, between us, we hatched a plan to catch the killer.
In essence, this would start with me dropping some loaded hints to
each of the main suspects in the course of the evening. Then, when
it was dark, I would announce to the group in general that I would
be taking Oscar for a walk around the estate, hoping that the
murderer would take the opportunity to creep out after me to
assault me. In preparation for this, Rocky would open the back
gate and the sergeant and her team would slip in unseen by the

guests and take up positions at strategic points around the garden, waiting for me to come out and, hopefully, for the murderer to pounce. The sergeant herself would take up station at the top of the pseudo Leaning Tower, armed with night-vision glasses, from where she could control the operation and speak to me in an earpiece that she would surreptitiously hand to me when she returned my passport.

It wasn't perfect but it would have to do.

At seven-thirty, Oscar and I went over to the kitchen to take Rocky and Antonella into my confidence. In order for the plan to work, I knew I needed their help and I felt sure I could count on them. I was pleased to find that Emile had gone out into the garden for a breath of fresh air and so I had the two of them to myself. After asking Rocky if he could make sure the back gate was once more unbolted, I asked the two of them to do a bit of play-acting for me and they nodded eagerly. Antonella, in particular, definitely looked up for the challenge.

'Just tell us what you'd like us to do, Dan.'

I gave her a big smile. 'Thanks, Antonella. It's like this: I'm going to try and convince each of my suspects that they're about to be arrested and that the only way out is for them to silence me.' I saw the same expression of alarm appear on her face as I had seen on Anna's and I did my best to sound reassuring. 'Once Rocky has opened the gate, the police are going to be positioned around the garden so I shouldn't be in any serious danger.' I hoped I was right but I didn't have much choice, so I adopted what I assumed would sound like a confident tone and continued. 'What I want you two to do is to plant suspicion in the minds of the two Swiss people. Did you know that Frau Baumgartner speaks Italian?' They both shook their heads. 'In fact, her Italian's very fluent but she doesn't know that you know that, so I want the two of you to engineer a situation where you are close enough for her to be able to overhear what you're saying, but where she believes that you've no idea she has understood. Is that clear?'

Antonella nodded eagerly. 'How exciting. Of course we can do that, can't we, Rocky?'

The man mountain nodded in agreement. 'What do you want us to say, Dan?'

I had given this a lot of thought and I consulted my notebook. 'You can choose your own words but what I want you to do is to have a whispered conversation – just loud enough for her to hear – in which you say that you've heard from me that I think they're the culprits and that first thing in the morning, I'll be heading off to the police station to spell out my suspicions to the sergeant. That way, with any luck, they'll be hauled off to prison. Do you think you can do that?'

Antonella and Rocky exchanged glances before she nodded decisively. 'Of course, Dan. Leave it to us.' A brief conversation then ensued between the two of them before she launched into a performance. Before starting, she pointed across the room at the fridge and added a little bit of stage direction for my benefit.

'Let's say the fridge is the Swiss couple.' She turned to her husband and adopted a stage whisper, loud enough for me and the fridge to hear. 'Look, Rocky, that's them there. Careful, don't let them see you looking at them. You heard what Dan said: first thing in the morning, the police should have locked them up.'

'Did they really kill Signor Farmer?' I could see that Rocky was entering into the spirit of the thing and his tone was suitably shocked.

'That's what Dan said. The stupid inspector didn't want to know, but he says the sergeant's much more receptive. He said he should get proof overnight and then he's heading to the *questura* first thing in the morning to hand it over to the sergeant. Then it'll be curtains for our Swiss friends.' After aiming a dirty look at the unresponsive fridge, she turned towards me and spoke in normal tones. 'Is that the sort of thing you wanted, Dan?'

'Perfect. Shakespeare couldn't have done it better.'

I thanked them both and put a tick alongside the two Swiss names in my notebook. Accompanied by my Labrador, who was unsurprisingly reluctant to leave the source of so much good food and who kept casting longing looks over his shoulder towards the kitchen, I walked around to the terrace to search for my next candidates for a bit of disinformation. I found Eugenie out on the lawn, talking on her phone, so I hurried across to her and when she saw me coming, she immediately rang off and turned towards me.

'Any developments?' Tonight, she was wearing a diaphanous white dress whose open neckline extended almost down to her waist.

I adopted a suitably grave tone. 'I'm not sure, but it's not looking good for Gus Cornish.'

She looked amazed. 'Gus?' There was disbelief in her voice. 'Are you trying to say that you think he killed Farmer? I would think he'd have trouble killing a fly. What makes you say that?'

'I'm in the process of working it out but I'm increasingly convinced that he is our murderer, possibly aided and abetted by Antoine Dujardin.'

'You must be joking.' She sounded completely dismissive. 'But why? What possible reason might they have for killing Farmer?'

'Revenge, Eugenie, plain and simple. It's looking increasingly as though both of them lost a lot of money to a financial scam run by the victim.' I took a melodramatic look around, checking we weren't being overheard, so as to add weight to my words. 'I just wanted you to know that I'm giving all the facts to the police first thing in the morning and one or both of them might well be arrested as a result. I'd advise you to get away from here as soon as possible so you don't get caught up in it.'

I left her there and went back towards the villa and I was delighted to find Piers out on the terrace on his own, so I put plan M into operation.

'Hi, Piers, I'm glad I've found you.' I deliberately kept my voice low and added a few cautious glances over my shoulder for good measure. 'I may have some bad news for you.'

'Why, what's happened? It's not Melanie, is it? She's all right, isn't she?'

His evident concern for her only served to reinforce what I had already guessed, so I hastened to capitalise on his obvious affection for his boss's wife. 'Yes, she's okay... for now. The thing is, it's looking very likely that either Melanie or Malcolm might be our murderer.'

He looked aghast. 'What, you think they killed Farmer? That's crazy...' His eyes were almost bulging out of his head and I decided to add a little bit of melodrama.

'Keep your voice down, Piers.' I did a quick 360-degree scan of the terrace to reinforce the message that this was a big secret. 'Did you know that she and Farmer were at university together?' It didn't need the slight shake of his head to indicate that this was news to him. 'Something happened back at Oxford all those years ago, and I'm waiting to hear from friends at Scotland Yard exactly what it was, and it's looking as though that might well provide a motive for murder.'

'Murder? You can't be serious, not Melanie...'

'I'll know definitely in the morning. Anyway, I wanted to give you a bit of advance warning so if you see her or Malcolm being marched off by the police, you'll know why.' At that moment, Eleanor Leonard appeared at the French windows so I dropped my voice to little more than a sinister hiss. 'Anyway, keep this to yourself, Piers. All right?'

I didn't give him time to do more than nod blankly. I was quite sure the first thing he would do would be to run to his beloved Melanie to reveal what I had just said and she, hopefully, would then relay it to Malcolm. Two birds with one stone.

I went across to Eleanor and adopted the same secretive approach. 'Good evening, Eleanor, I need to talk to you. Would you mind coming with me for a little stroll?'

Accompanied by Oscar, we walked down the steps and along the gravel path as far as the lawn. By now, Eugenie had disappeared, hopefully to tell Antoine – and by extension, Gus – what I had just told her a few moments earlier. When we were a discreet distance from the house, I turned towards Eleanor, still doing my best to sound as mysterious as possible. 'Just a quiet word in your ear. My contacts at Scotland Yard say that the security services are very worried about some of your husband's business dealings and there's the suspicion that Farmer might have known something incriminating about him. I'll know more by first thing tomorrow and I'll report it to the police as soon as I hear.'

Her beautiful eyes opened wide. 'What are you saying? Surely you don't think my husband could be involved in murder?'

'Him personally, no, but he has some very unsavoury friends.' I let my expression harden. 'But you already know that, don't you?' I saw a hint of acknowledgement in her eyes and pressed on. 'I wouldn't want you to become collateral damage, so I strongly advise you to leave the villa just as soon as you can. I understand from the police that they'll be returning your travel documents to you all later tonight.' I tapped the side of my nose with my finger and gave her a knowing look. 'Just a word to the wise: leave here first thing in the morning before this all turns very nasty.'

I left her there looking thoroughly bamboozled and made a quick circuit of the garden with Oscar before returning to the terrace. It came as no surprise to find that Piers had also disappeared – quite likely busily relating to Melanie what I had told him

– and his place had been taken by Gus Cornish. He was still looking as suave as ever but what I had to say to him next definitely wiped the smile off his face.

'Hi, Gus, I'm glad I caught you. Antoine Dujardin has probably told you that I know about you and him.' It looked as if he was going to say something but I held up my hand to stop him. 'That's your personal business and nothing to do with anybody else but I just wanted to warn you that it looks as though he might be involved with Farmer's murder.'

His suntanned face positively blanched. 'Antoine? Surely not. He couldn't be involved in something like murder. Besides, why would he have wanted to kill Farmer?'

'It's a money thing. I'm investigating a rumour that Antoine lost millions in a scam run by Farmer.'

'Do you have proof?'

I shook my head. 'Not quite yet, but I should know more in the next few hours. The problem I have is that the police here aren't interested and unless I can convince them when I see them first thing tomorrow morning, an innocent woman is going to end up in prison.'

'That's terrible, but surely not Antoine...' His voice tailed off in bewilderment and I added a little more.

'That's what it's looking like.' The sound of voices behind me made me drop my voice even lower. 'Anyway, not a word to Antoine. All right?'

I turned and saw the other guests starting to emerge from the French windows for their dinner. I headed for them, determined at all costs to ensure that I didn't let any of them get me on my own, either to object to what I'd been suggesting, or to take immediate drastic action to silence me.

It looked like being quite an evening.

23

WEDNESDAY EVENING

The atmosphere at dinner was tense. I deliberately positioned myself with Piers to my right and Gus Cornish to my left and did my best to ignore any queries they might level at me about my suspicions. I could see eyes around the table staring at me, some in amazement and some with open hostility.

In particular, Frau Baumgartner looked as though she was about to blow a fuse. There was a vein just above her right eye visibly throbbing and I could see she was in the grip of high emotion – whether this was outrage, indignation or murderous intent remained to be seen. I could just see the side of Antoine's face beyond Gus and I noticed that he had developed a nervous tic in his cheek. On the other side of me, Melanie studiously avoided my gaze and hardly said a word all meal. Opposite her, Eugenie was clearly more reserved than usual and barely spoke to anybody. I wondered whether she had told Antoine what I'd said, and whether he and Gus had spoken about it. I certainly hoped so.

The only two people who appeared relatively untouched by the general mood of suspicion and uncertainty were Malcolm Derby and Erich Baumgartner. They were sitting side by side and were chatting in a remarkably relaxed manner. The fact that Erich always appeared to have a glass in his hand was probably helping to relax him – although I felt I could still detect an underlying air of concern, or more – while Malcolm was clearly doing his best to generate some good cheer around the table but without much success. From his relatively relaxed attitude, I assumed that if Piers had told Melanie of my suspicions about her past with Farmer, she maybe hadn't told her husband. All in all, however, there was a general mood of fear and suspicion among most of my companions around the table. My plan of shaking things up appeared to be working. The big question now was whether the murderer would take the bait.

It was another outstanding meal but, under the circumstances, I wondered how many people appreciated it. Steadfastly trying to shrug off any thoughts of a condemned man eating a hearty breakfast, I did my best to do justice to Emile's latest *chef-d'oeuvre*. Tonight, our starters were scallops in their shells flambéed with a brandy, goat cheese and cinnamon sauce. The result was spectacular. As a nod to our Italian location, he followed this with an exquisite seafood risotto before the main course. Tonight, the main attraction looked mightily impressive as Rocky brought in a silver platter almost a metre long. On this was a huge fish, the size of a salmon, that Emile had steamed and then meticulously skinned and deboned before covering it with slivers of cucumber to look like scales. I'm not sure what the fish was called but it had white flesh rather than the pink of salmon and the taste was delightful. Served with a salad of fennel, quails' eggs and smoked lardons, it had to be one of the best fish dishes I had ever tasted.

All the way through the meal, I was waiting anxiously for somebody to look across the table and start accusing me of rumour-mongering or worse but, thankfully, nobody went down that road. Hopefully, they were all still unaware that I had been levelling accusations at each of them individually and so presumably they were worried about revealing such matters in front of the others for fear of losing face. As for the actual murderer, I repeatedly scanned the faces around me but was unable to put my finger on anybody in particular.

It was at just before ten o'clock, as I was enjoying Emile's take on baked Alaska with a fruits-of-the-forest coulis, that Sergeant Innocenti arrived with everybody's travel documents. She walked around the table handing these out until she reached me. As I took mine from her, she swept her briefcase in front of me and I felt a little packet containing the communication device she had promised me land in my lap. As the time for action approached, it was reassuring to know that the plan was being carried out perfectly. So far...

She didn't stay long, just long enough to thank everybody for their patience and cooperation, and then she left again. While I was finishing my dessert and waiting for my double espresso to arrive, I could visualise her and her people moving in around the outside of the estate through the little gate and taking up position in readiness for the next stage of this evening's attempt to trap the killer. So far, nobody had left the table but when I saw Frau Baumgartner get to her feet and give her husband a peremptory tap on the shoulder, I hastened to put my part of the plan into operation. Draining the last of my coffee, I stood up as well and announced to the table at large that Oscar and I were going for our evening walk in the garden. With that, I hurried away down the steps before anybody could accost me or follow me.

Away from the lights of the villa, it was pitch dark out there, and it took me a couple of minutes before my eyes adjusted fully and I was able to see reasonably well. It was too early for the moon, and the stars were just beginning to sparkle above me, but they didn't cast much light. I kept glancing back towards the terrace and saw that it had rapidly emptied. The only figures I could see now were Antonella and Rocky as they cleared the table. This might mean simply that everybody had retired into the villa or it could mean that the murderer was already out on the prowl, determined to silence me. It was an uncomfortable feeling knowing that I was the bait in a potentially lethal trap but I knew it was all I had left to try. More importantly, this might be the only way to save my girlfriend's daughter from jail. Any amount of jeopardy for me had to be worthwhile to avoid that, surely. Although my pragmatic side told me this was the only course of action open to me, pragmatism didn't do much to slow my racing pulse.

It occurred to me, almost for the first time, that instead of a physical assault at close quarters with a knife or club, I might find myself in the night sights of a killer with a sniper's rifle. No sooner had this thought crossed my mind than I did my best to dismiss it – but it wasn't easy. I reminded myself that the police had searched the villa from top to bottom two days earlier so it was surely impossible for one of my dinner companions to have secreted a large weapon. There did, however, always remain the possibility, however unlikely, that Farmer's killer had come in from outside and might be back again, ready to commit murder – only this time, the target would be me.

I carefully scanned every bush, tree and shrub as Oscar and I took a long, slow tour of the grounds. I hadn't realised before just how silent it was here within the high brick walls. I could hear the crunch of my feet on the gravel of the path and I could even hear Oscar's breath. Fireflies among the branches of the trees kept me turning my head but, for now, I saw nobody.

'Jesus!'

The silence had suddenly been broken by a crackling in my ear and the sound of Paola's voice coming through the earpiece remarkably clearly. I freely admit that the noise made me jump and I realised just how tense I had become.

'Dan, can you hear me?'

I kept my voice low as I murmured into the tiny mic. 'Perfectly, thanks. Nothing to report my end yet. What about you?'

'No, nothing except to reassure you that we're all in position. There are eight officers spread around so if anything happens, just shout and somebody will be with you in seconds.'

I thanked her and continued to walk slowly along the narrow path, nerves stretched and all my instincts telling me to be alert. As I did so, I let my mind range once more over the suspects I had before me. On Monday night, everybody had had opportunity to kill Farmer, many had had motive and the rack of daggers on the wall had provided easy means for a killer with a strong stomach. The question was, which of them had it been? If only Inspector Vinci had put in the inquiries immediately on Tuesday morning, we might by now have a better idea of any possible financial or personal connections between the guests here and Monday's victim. Still, even without knowing the full facts, I gradually came around to the conclusion that my number one suspect probably had to be Frau Birgit Baumgartner.

No sooner had this thought crystallised in my head than I questioned my reasoning. To my mind, she was a most unpleasant individual but being unpleasant doesn't necessarily make you a killer. I had little doubt that, given the opportunity, she would probably have had the balls to stab Farmer, which was more than could be said about her jovial, drunken husband. Or was it? Thought of him suddenly reminded me of something Antonella had said. On that first night when Erich had apparently been trying to drink the villa's cellar dry, Antonella had told me that when she was clearing up afterwards, she had had to mop the terrace floor beneath his chair because it had been awash with spilt wine. Spilt or deliberately poured there so as to surreptitiously empty his glass? Had Erich's excessive consumption of alcohol been a smokescreen to disguise the fact that he had been anything but drunk and incapable? Could it be that the jovial exterior of the Swiss financier concealed a far more sinister character beneath?

I carried on walking, occasionally picking up a stick and throwing it for Oscar to retrieve but doing my best to concentrate on what lay ahead of me and also on what or who might be behind me. I was constantly swivelling my head to the left and right and even walking backwards for a few steps so as to check that nobody was coming up on me unseen. Oscar proceeded with his walk unperturbed and I took solace in the fact that he didn't seem bothered by the shadows. If somebody had been lurking, I hoped he would have reacted but, unless it happened to be a squirrel, this might well have been a forlorn hope.

The path gradually skirted around the lawn and passed the mass of bushes that concealed the back gate until it reached Thomas Gregory's replica Leaning Tower. I took a seat on the bench at the foot of this for a few minutes, glad of a break. Knowing that the sergeant was concealed directly above me was comforting, as was the feel of the solid wall behind my back. I gradually let my breathing slow and my heart rate return to something approaching normal. I could feel the cold sweat starting to dry on my back and I wiped my sticky palms on my trousers. Walking around in the dark, waiting for a killer to leap out with a knife or worse, is a stressful pastime, and I knew I'd be very happy when it was over.

After a while, I murmured into the microphone. 'No luck so far. I'll do one more circuit now and then we'll just have to accept that the experiment has failed.' I did my best to keep the disappointment out of my voice, but she must have picked it up all the same.

'Understood, but it's not over yet. Keep your eyes open and remember that we're all around you.'

I got to my feet and set off back along the path again. Although Oscar and I were out for another twenty minutes, the result was the same. We met nobody and nobody tried to assault me. It was clear that the killer hadn't taken the bait after all. As I walked back towards the lights of the villa, it was with mixed feelings. On the one hand, I had to confess to feeling relieved no longer to be risking my life, but on the other, there was natural disappointment at a plan not working. Along with this came the dawning realisation that unless a miracle happened in the next few hours, all of my suspects were going to leave, and things would look truly bleak for Virginia.

24

WEDNESDAY NIGHT

Sergeant Innocenti dismissed her officers and came back with me to my apartment over the old stables. I had been careful to lock the door at the bottom of the stairs before going out but I still checked every nook and cranny of the place before returning to the kitchenette and offering Paola a drink. She thanked me but shook her head.

'I should've been home hours ago so I really need to get back to the family. I'm so sorry the plan didn't work. We knew we were taking a chance because the murderer hasn't put a foot out of place so far. And, of course, now that the people here have their passports back, I'm sure there's going to be a general exodus first thing in the morning.'

I nodded gloomily. 'I'm sure you're right. At least from your point of view, you already have a suspect in custody and enough evidence to proceed, even if it's just with a charge of involuntary manslaughter in self-defence.' Although the fact that the murder weapon had deliberately been brought from downstairs would appear to indicate intent, but I didn't mention that. No doubt a smart prosecutor would soon pick up on that and it wouldn't help

Virginia's chances. 'I just feel very sorry for Virginia because I'm ever more convinced of her innocence.' I caught the sergeant's eye. 'And I'm not just saying that because I have a family connection to her. Whoever murdered Farmer went to a lot of trouble to cover their tracks and to incriminate Rocky with the Rolex, as well as opening the back gate to throw suspicion away from the villa inhabitants. I'm still convinced that it's somebody here and my money is ever more definitely on the Swiss couple.'

I went on to tell her about the pool of wine beneath Erich's chair on the first night and she nodded. 'Yes, that *is* interesting. I'll speak to my superiors first thing in the morning and see if they would be prepared to let me haul Mr and Mrs Baumgartner into the *questura* for a serious questioning session, in the hope that one of them cracks.' She caught my eye and shook her head ruefully. 'But I wouldn't count on it. If it is one of them, they've been covering their tracks well up till now.'

'Too true, but I definitely think it's worth a try. I'll be up early and I'll make sure I keep them here until I hear from you. I just hope your superiors agree. The Baumgartners are important people and, by the sound of it, the Minister for Justice is interested in this case now, so he might well take the easy option and stick with the prisoner you already have.' I went on to thank Paola most warmly for all her help and cooperation, in spite of the negative result. I told her that if I'd still been in the force, I would have been delighted to have somebody like her serving alongside me.

She blushed and thanked me before leaving me with a warning. 'You should be pretty secure up here on the first floor but just make sure you keep the door locked tonight. You never know, the killer may still have you in their sights. Call me if you need me. You have my number. *Ciao*, Dan.'

After Paola had left, I opened a few windows to let some cooler air in as it felt stuffy in here, but my rational self told me this was probably just me still getting over the stress of the past hour. I poured myself a glass of cold, white wine from the fridge and settled down on the sofa, taking a few long, soothing breaths. After turning off the lights to deter any mosquitoes, I sat back, trying to think myself into the head of the murderer. Maybe my plan had been too naïve. Would Farmer's killer really have considered it worth risking yet another murder inquiry in order to silence the person they viewed as their biggest danger? Obviously, another murder while Virginia was locked up would have cast serious doubt on the validity of her arrest and would have effectively put the investigation back to square one. Regretfully, I had to admit that, in spite of my hopes, if I had been in the killer's shoes, I would probably have taken the risk of any fresh evidence being too weak to affect things and just got the hell out of here as soon as I could.

I looked at my watch and checked the time. Remarkably, it was only just after eleven o'clock. Somehow, it felt like the depths of the night. I sent a text to Anna, telling her that the plan was now in operation and that I was all right. After that, I texted Rocky, asking him if any of the guests had already opted to leave tonight, and two minutes later, I received the unwelcome news that the Baumgartners had called a taxi immediately after dinner and left, although all the others had opted to spend one more night at the villa before leaving in the morning. I sat looking helplessly at the message on my phone. Now my two prime suspects had just left and were probably already on their way back to Switzerland and quite probably with them went my hopes of a happy ending for poor Virginia. I toyed with the idea of texting Paola to see if they could be stopped at the airport or the station but, without any kind of evidence against them, I knew that there was no chance of this being authorised so I didn't bother.

I sat there in the dark turning the case over and over again in my head but each time being forced to accept the unwelcome conclusion that the only person against whom there was any kind of solid evidence was Virginia. I could only begin to imagine the effect a court appearance and a trial would have on her and on her mother. It would be devastating for both of them and, not to mention for me.

Gradually, as the minutes ticked by, I must have dozed off and I was woken by repeated prods of my leg from a cold wet nose. The moon had risen by now and I could see Oscar's eyes glowing green in the reflected light. I checked my watch and saw that it was almost three o'clock. I looked down at him, wondering if he was trying to tell me that he needed a comfort break, when he turned away and trotted towards the bedroom door. It was closed and he wasn't able to get inside but I saw him reach out with a front paw and start scratching at the woodwork. My dozy brain slowly started working again and a shot of adrenaline suddenly flashed through me. Had Oscar heard something? Had somebody got into the house?

I slipped off my shoes, stood up and padded silently to the bedroom door, pausing en route to pick up an African sculpture from a side table. It was a skilful representation of a tall, slim man and it had, from my point of view, the particular attraction of having a solid, heavy base. I reversed it in my hand so that I was holding the head and the statue formed an effective club, although I was under no illusion that if there was an intruder in the apartment with a firearm, a chunk of wood wouldn't do me much good.

When I got to the door, I stood and listened carefully, trying to work out what Oscar had heard. His nose was at the crack of the door and his hackles had risen. This in itself was so unusual for my normally easy-going dog that I gripped the statue even more firmly. I reached for the handle, knowing that I was going to look pretty silly if I opened the door to find that one of the local cats had climbed in through the open window. I took a deep breath and started to turn it.

What happened next was a blur. The door was suddenly kicked open in my face, sending me backwards and making me slip and fall to one knee. As I did so, a figure leapt towards me and I could see the moonlight glistening on the end of a vicious steel blade. I was still trying to regain my balance when salvation, in the shape of my four-legged friend, intervened. Oscar gave an unusually ferocious growl and jumped towards my assailant, shielding me with his body as the man charged me, with the result that my would-be assassin tripped over sixty pounds of currently overfed canine bone and muscle and sprawled headlong onto the floor. By this time, I was back on my feet and I threw myself onto the figure, pinning him to the floor with my knee in the small of his back. I caught hold of his left arm and twisted it up behind his back while with my free hand, I caught hold of the arm still holding the knife and smashed the knuckles of the hand repeatedly onto the wooden floor until the knife flew free and I heard it clatter against the fireplace.

The man squirmed beneath me but in vain. I knew I was well in control now. This wasn't a muscleman like Rocky, but a very different beast. In the moonlight, I had already worked out that this was a sixty-one-year-old Swiss financier called Erich. I looked up and saw the green glow of my dog's eyes. He was standing a few feet away, looking remarkably attentive, and I gave him a little smile.

'Thanks, dog. That's another one I owe you.'

He definitely smiled back at me.

I waited until Baumgartner gave up struggling before addressing him, his left arm still yanked up behind his back and my knee still pinning him to the ground.

'Good evening, Erich. I've been waiting for you.'

No sooner had I said it than it struck me that this had to be one of the corniest lines I could have chosen. This wasn't a thriller and I wasn't 007 and, had it not been for my dog, I might well be lying dead now with a dagger in my heart just like Jonathan Farmer. I let my voice harden and added a bit more weight to the knee in his back. 'You had me fooled; you had us all fooled. We were all convinced you were hopelessly drunk on Monday night when all the time, you were planning a gruesome murder.'

'Please get your knee out of my back and let go of my arm. You're hurting me. Ouch.' He was squealing in pain and my first impression was that this didn't sound like the voice of a dedicated killer.

I released the pressure a tad but kept as much menace in my voice as I could. 'Good, I'm glad it hurts. Think yourself lucky that I don't break your arm. I'm not in the police force any longer so I don't need to play by the rules.' Even as I said it, I found myself cringing at the Hollywood cliché, but I was determined to scare the living daylights out of him in order to get to the truth. 'Try to imagine just how much I hate and despise you. You were fully prepared to let an innocent girl go to prison for the murder you committed and you tried to put the blame on Rocky by dropping Farmer's watch in his coat pocket. You didn't care who you killed and you didn't care who you framed. All you were thinking about was yourself.'

He gave no response and just lay there. From the movement of his shoulders, I got the impression that he might even be sobbing. Again, hardly the reaction I would have expected from a cold-blooded killer who had so callously and clinically stabbed Farmer to death face to face. I began to smell a rat. Maybe Erich the murderer wasn't quite what he seemed.

First things first, I spent the next five minutes awkwardly removing my belt with my free hand and lashing his wrists together. He made no attempt to resist and I could hear him sobbing quietly. It was only a temporary fix but it allowed me to stand up. I left him lying face down on the floor, switched on the light and then came back until I was in his line of sight and brandished the African statue at him.

'You're going to lie there, Erich, and you aren't going to move. If you do, I'll come over and knock you senseless. Be warned.'

One look at his tear-stained face told me that I would have no need of my improvised club. He looked completely overcome, beaten, distraught. Over the years in the police, I had been present at the capture of a number of murderers, but seeing somebody so recently armed and determined to kill go so completely to pieces was unusual to say the least. My suspicions deepened even more.

I picked up my phone and called Paola. I could have phoned the *questura* without disturbing her, but I knew how much it would mean to her for this arrest to be hers. She sounded sleepy when she answered the phone, but she was wide awake in seconds. All the time that I was explaining to her what had happened, I kept my eyes on the man on the floor but he just stayed where he was, staring helplessly sideways into space. As soon as the call ended, I remembered my other priorities and did two things. First, I grabbed my dog and gave him a warm hug of gratitude – receiving a slobbery lick in return – and then I sent a one-line text to Anna saying simply:

Murderer caught thanks to Oscar. All good. X

25

EARLY THURSDAY MORNING

I dug out my one and only tie and did a better job of lashing Baumgartner's wrists together and then used my belt to secure his feet, effectively immobilising him, although throughout the whole process, he made no attempt to struggle or free himself. I hauled him up, sat him on the sofa, and took a seat on a chair opposite him. I put my phone on the coffee table between us and pressed the voice record button, determined to do this by the book – just like old times.

Baumgartner made a pathetic sight. The tears had stopped but he was as white as a sheet and I could see his lower lip trembling with emotion. Paola had told me she and her officers would be here in the next fifteen minutes or so, and that might just give me time to get to the bottom of what was happening. I owed it to Virginia – if not myself – to discover the truth. I had little doubt that if it had been Inspector Vinci conducting the interrogation, he would have gone straight to bad-cop mode – did he have another mode? – but, instead, I adopted a more conciliatory tone.

'Want to tell me all about it, Erich?' He made no response so I started with a practical question. 'How did you manage to get into my bedroom?'

This, at least, caught his attention, and for a moment, he made eye contact with me. 'A ladder. There was a ladder in the old stables downstairs.'

That explained that, and I gave myself a mental kicking. The very least I should have done was to have checked all means of access. Was this the onset of old age kicking in? Inconsequentially, it occurred to me that my fifty-seventh birthday was coming up in less than a month's time. Was I, to paraphrase the immortal words of the Hollywood blockbuster movie, *getting too old for this stuff*? Doing my best to shrug off thoughts of my impending descent into decrepitude, I looked across at Erich and tried again.

'I heard that you and your wife had left. How did you come back here?'

'Rented car.' His voice was low and I could barely hear him.

'What on earth did you think you were doing? You know you could go to prison now for the rest of your life, don't you?' I glanced across at the dagger lying in the fireplace and saw that it was yet another taken from the collection on the wall of the music room. 'What made you come here tonight and what made you kill Farmer?' His eyes dropped back to his feet again but, just before they did, I glimpsed a spark in them and suddenly, the clouds in my head parted and with a dazzling flash, I realised that I had been right all along. 'No, that's the wrong question. I should have asked you *who* made you come here tonight, shouldn't I?'

He kept his eyes trained on his feet and gave no response but I felt pretty sure I knew where I was going now, so I tried again. 'What was it you said in your interview with the police? Fifteen years of happy marriage, I seem to remember. Just how happy *is* your marriage, Erich?' There was still no reaction, so I ramped it up a notch. 'How did you end up married to somebody like her?

You're a nice guy; you're sociable and have a sense of humour. What could you possibly have in common with Birgit?'

Maybe it was my use of his wife's first name that did it, but he slowly raised his eyes from the floor. They were bloodshot and red-rimmed – hardly the eyes of a killer. 'Money, that's what.'

I made no comment and waited patiently for him to continue. It felt like an age but in fact, it was probably only half a minute before he started speaking again. 'Does the name Lehman Brothers mean anything to you? The 2008 financial crisis?'

I couldn't recall the detail but I certainly remembered the infamous name and the financial crash and I nodded at Erich. He didn't appear to notice and he just continued to talk.

'My company was doing really well until then and suddenly, almost overnight, I was bankrupt. Can you imagine how that feels? One minute, I'm flying across the Atlantic first class, the next, I'm moving into a two-room rented flat at the butt end of Zurich.' There was real bitterness in his voice now. 'Birgit bailed me out...'

'And that's why you married her?'

'What choice did I have? I'm not good with poverty, and you get used to money, you see. By marrying her, I got back on the ladder.'

'At the expense of your personal happiness.'

He actually caught my eye for once. There was an almost pleading look in it. 'My personal happiness demands money first of all. I know that makes me sound shallow and I know I am, but the money made me happy and the money made our marriage bearable.' What could have been a hint of a rueful smile flitted across his face for a fraction of a second. 'And the drink helps. A lot.'

It was all becoming clear now but I did my best to tread lightly. 'So are you telling me that on Monday night, it wasn't an act? When I saw you staggering about, was that because you really were drunk?'

He gave the slightest of nods. 'Like I say, it helps.'

'So what really happened on Monday night?'

'I honestly can't remember. I can vaguely recall going upstairs to the room and then nothing until early next morning.'

He looked so broken that I had little doubt that he was telling the truth. The question was whether, in spite of having been so drunk, he had still somehow managed to murder Farmer or whether, in fact, Farmer had been murdered by somebody else. And there were no prizes for guessing who that might have been. What I now needed from Erich was confirmation of my suspicions.

'And where is Birgit now?'

'Outside in the car. Just down the road.'

Before continuing the questions, I sent a quick text to Paola.

Frau B in rented car nearby. Arrest her.

Returning my attention to Erich, I tried another line of inquiry. 'When did you first learn that Farmer had been murdered?'

'Birgit told me early on Tuesday morning. She woke me up at dawn to tell me.'

'And did she say who did it?'

There was a long pause and then he gave a resigned nod. 'She told me *I* did it.'

'And did you?'

An agonised expression spread across his face. 'I don't know. I can't remember. I honestly can't believe that I'd be capable of doing something like that, but that's what she said.'

'And what reason did she give for the murder?'

'That's easy. Just over a year ago, Farmer screwed us out of millions and the company lost almost half its assets. We're surviving, but only just. The hardest thing has been trying to keep it a secret. If it had got out that we'd been scammed, our credibility would have gone out of the window and we would have been ruined. It was a scheme being marketed by a company in the BVI that we subsequently discovered to be one of Farmer's subsidiaries. We knew it was risky but the returns were potentially enormous. What we didn't realise at the time was that he was behind it and just what sort of cheating scumbag he really was. When it all fell apart, he came out of it with millions in the bank while we and all the other investors were left with next to nothing.' His voice was stronger now. 'I'll be completely honest: hearing that he was dead was the best news I've had for months.'

'But it came as news to *you*, the supposed murderer? Are you seriously expecting me to believe that you were so drunk, you don't remember doing it, but you were sober enough to have been able to stab him clinically in exactly the right position to stop his heart instantly?' He just shook his head helplessly so I continued. 'And what about tonight? You're certainly not falling-over drunk this time. What made you decide you were suddenly going to turn into a killer, or have you been telling me a pack of lies and you know full well what you did on Monday night?'

This time, I had to wait almost a minute for him to reply. When he finally answered, his voice was flat, expressionless. 'Birgit said we had to liquidate you before you found out the truth. She said the police here had already wound up their investigation and, seeing as I'd already committed one murder, it would be easy for me to commit a second. She stole the knife before we left the villa so that suspicion would fall on people still here.' He looked up for a moment. 'She's a very organised, methodical person. She came up with the idea of dropping Farmer's Rolex into a random coat pocket to deviate attention and she even went poking around in the bushes until she found the back gate to open so the police would think the murderer had come from outside.'

An expression of anguish flooded his face as he continued.

'She's a strong woman. Not like me. I was trembling so much when I was climbing the ladder to get in your window, I almost fell off. When I was in the bedroom and I could hear your dog scratching at the door, I nearly passed out with fear. What I don't understand is how I managed to kill Farmer when I can hardly bring myself to kill a spider.'

I nodded a few times before deciding to just go for it. 'Hasn't it occurred to you, Erich, that maybe you didn't kill Farmer after all?'

'But Birgit said I did...' He was almost wailing now.

'Think it through, Erich. The only way you know you killed Farmer is because your wife told you so. Ask yourself this: how did she know at dawn on Tuesday morning that Farmer was dead? You were dead drunk and asleep and Antonella didn't discover the body until a couple of hours later. How did your wife know?'

I sat and waited patiently while I saw him slowly working his way around to the obvious conclusion. The unmistakable sound of powerful engines in the distance became louder and louder as I began to read comprehension on his face and he looked up at me in disbelief.

'Are you saying *she* did it? You mean *I* didn't...?' There was awe in his voice. 'Surely, she wouldn't...?'

'She wouldn't what, Erich? She wouldn't murder Farmer or she wouldn't stoop to making her harmless drunk of a husband believe he was a killer and then send him out to kill again?' I heard the sound of vehicles pulling up outside and I stared down at him for a moment. 'I'm afraid you're going to have a lot of time on your hands over the next few years to ask yourself those questions. Good luck, Erich, you're going to need it.'

In spite of the fact that he had come here to kill me – and, without the intervention of my four-legged friend, he might well have succeeded – I felt a twinge of pity for this broken man.

For his wife, I felt no pity whatsoever.

EPILOGUE
THURSDAY LUNCHTIME

Lunch on Thursday was a joyous occasion and not just because Emile surpassed himself with an open buffet groaning with everything from cold lobster, a huge steaming pot of moules marinière, scallops au gratin and some of the finest cold roast beef I had ever tasted. Accompanied by no fewer than five different salads ranging from a very Gallic take on coleslaw to a wonderful mixture of rocket leaves, black olives and quails' eggs, as well as fresh green asparagus tips covered with a blue-cheese sauce, followed by a selection of mouth-watering desserts, it was a true celebration feast. It went without saying that Gus insisted it be accompanied by some very good champagne.

Around the table were the surviving remnants of Malcolm Derby's ill-fated meeting, along with Anna and a very happy Virginia, whose first act upon seeing me had been to hug me as if her life depended on it. At least one positive had come out of the tragic events of this week.

The mood around the table was one of overwhelming relief. I had gone to each of the residents in turn in the course of the morning to explain why I had made my Machiavellian insinuations the previous night and to apologise for any concerns these might have raised. I had been delighted to find that they had all understood my motives and appeared to forgive me. Malcolm Derby had been most complimentary and he had the decency to confess to his mistake.

'I've told Piers to make sure that any future potential investors are cleaner than clean. I must admit to having been so keen to get things moving that I didn't vet these participants well enough.'

'You could hardly be expected to anticipate murder.' I shook my head in disbelief. 'Although the more I learn about Farmer, the dodgier he sounds.'

He nodded. 'Like I say, Dan, the GS Flight project is a potentially global undertaking and we need to take our time and find the right people. And on that subject, I'm eternally grateful that you came along to help. Without you, an innocent woman might well have ended up in jail.' He raised his glass towards Virginia and her mother alongside me. 'I couldn't be happier for you all. Cheers.'

His wife raised her own glass and gave me a big smile. 'Having you here has been like being in our very own murder mystery, Dan. Good luck with your next book.'

At my request, we were joined for lunch by Sergeant Innocenti, who also gave me a most unprofessional hug when she saw me, but who was I to complain? As for Anna, she had absolutely showered me with kisses and Oscar was looking positively jealous by the time she released me.

The police had found the rented car and arrested Frau Baumgartner the previous night and Paola was able to tell us that at formal interview this morning, Erich had repeated his story incriminating his wife. Birgit Baumgartner herself, on the other hand, had steadfastly refused to utter a single word. Fortunately, a forensic examination of the long evening gloves she had been wearing on Monday night had revealed microscopic traces of blood that were being analysed as we spoke. Paola told us that the prosecutor was happy to see both of them go to trial and it looked as though they would be safely locked up for years to come. Unexpectedly, when details had arrived that morning of Farmer's will, it was discovered that almost all of his personal and business wealth would go to the foundation of a trust to *nurture and support outstanding talent in the field of economics*. I hoped that beneficiaries of this foundation would turn out to have a bit more moral fibre than its patron.

At the end of the meal, I went through to the kitchen to thank Emile for the food, but also to thank Antonella and Rocky for their help in my investigation. Needless to say, I was accompanied by Oscar, who immediately feigned starvation. As usual, it worked, and he soon found himself on the receiving end of a piece of meat that would have fed a sizeable family. But, all things considered, as they say in the adverts, he's worth it.

Before returning to the *questura*, Paola took me to one side and whispered that she had been told that her promotion to inspector had now been approved and that she was replacing Adolfo Vinci with immediate effect. As for him, there were rumours going around that once he was back on his feet again, he was to be transferred to the port area of Gioia Tauro, far away in the south of Italy. I had already heard of this massive container port, allegedly firmly in the hands of Italy's nastiest organised crime clan, the 'Ndrangheta. I certainly didn't envy him the challenge – with or without a bazooka as a handgun.

Anna, Virginia and I took Oscar for a final stroll around the gardens and in comparison to my nerve-tingling circuit of the garden the previous night, it was wonderfully relaxing to savour the heady aroma of jasmine in the air and to admire the beauty of the luxuriant waves of deep purple bougainvillea spilling over the stone walls surrounding the lawn. Our walk led us to the pseudo tower and Oscar had no hesitation in nosing the door open and heading straight up the stairs, followed by the three of us. The sky was clear and the views in all directions impressive. In particular, the sun reflecting against the huge, white bulk of the duomo, the baptistery and, of course, the real leaning tower, made these magnificent monuments stand out against the deep green of the Apennines behind. It was very quiet up here, the only sound the gentle rustling of the leaves in the surrounding branches as the light breeze barely stirred them. I leant on the retaining wall and looked out over the beautiful formal gardens of Villa Gregory laid out below us, savouring the peace and quiet.

There was a movement at my feet and Oscar, ever curious, stood up on his back legs and peered over the wall beside me, his nose sniffing the breeze and his eyes scouring the surroundings. Seconds later, the peace of the afternoon was shattered as he spotted a squirrel, one of his sworn enemies, wandering casually along a branch just below us. For once, he found himself higher up than a squirrel and his excitement knew no bounds. He launched into a paroxysm of barking and was already scrabbling at the wall with his back paws, apparently readying himself for a kamikaze leap into the abyss, when Anna caught him by the collar and held him back.

'No, Oscar!' He stopped barking and glanced sideways at her as she wagged a finger at him. 'It's bad enough your master trying to get himself killed without you joining in.' She looked up at me and smiled. 'You're a bad influence on your dog.'

I hung my head in mock shame. 'Sorry, ma'am. I'll try to do better in future.'

I heard Virginia's voice at my ear. 'As far as I'm concerned, you couldn't have done any better. Thank you from the bottom of my heart, Dan.'

I grinned back at her as an overwhelming sensation of happiness and relief washed over me. I had come here dreading the prospect of finding that my girlfriend's only daughter would never want to acknowledge me or speak to me. How that might have impacted my relationship with Anna didn't bear thinking about. All right, almost getting myself killed was a radical way of resolving matters, but thankfully, everything had turned out all right in the end. I reached across and gave her hand a gentle squeeze.

'It was the least I could do but, just to keep your mum happy, I promise I won't attack any squirrels from now on.'

I glanced down and caught Oscar's eye. It was pretty clear that he wasn't prepared to promise anything of the sort. Still, considering he'd probably saved my life last night, he was entitled to bark at a squirrel from time to time. I gave him an affectionate smile.

'You're a good dog, Oscar.'

But, of course, he already knew that.

ACKNOWLEDGMENTS

Warmest thanks to my lovely editor, Emily Ruston at the excellent Boldwood Books, ably assisted by the hawkeyed Sue Smith and Emily Reader, the proofreader with the perfect name. Thanks to my friend John Smith for patiently accompanying me on an eighteen-kilometre route march around Pisa when I went back to refresh my memory of that beautiful city. Finally, thanks, as always, to Mariangela, my wife, who is always the first to read anything I write. Her comments and suggestions are invaluable, as is her expertise in Italian history, culture and language.

ABOUT THE AUTHOR

T. A. Williams is the author of over twenty bestselling romances for HQ and Canelo and is now turning his hand to cosy crime, set in his beloved Italy, for Boldwood. The series introduces us to to DCI Armstrong and his labrador Oscar. Trevor lives in Devon with his Italian wife.

Sign up to T. A. Williams' mailing list here for news, competitions and updates on future books.

Visit T. A. Williams' website: http://www.tawilliamsbooks.com

Follow T. A. Williams' on social media:

x.com/TAWilliamsBooks

facebook.com/TrevorWilliamsBooks

ALSO BY T. A. WILLIAMS

Poison
& Pens

POISON & PENS IS THE HOME OF
COZY MYSTERIES SO POUR YOURSELF
A CUP OF TEA & GET SLEUTHING!

DISCOVER PAGE–TURNING NOVELS FROM
YOUR FAVOURITE AUTHORS &
MEET NEW FRIENDS

JOIN OUR
FACEBOOK GROUP

BIT.LYPOISONANDPENSFB

SIGN UP TO OUR
NEWSLETTER

BIT.LY/POISONANDPENSNEWS

Boldwood

Boldwood Books is an award-winning fiction publishing company seeking out the best stories from around the world.

Find out more at www.boldwoodbooks.com

Join our reader community for brilliant books, competitions and offers!

Follow us
@BoldwoodBooks
@TheBoldBookClub

Sign up to our weekly deals newsletter

https://bit.ly/BoldwoodBNewsletter

Printed in Great Britain
by Amazon

38468956R00129